ABOUT THIS BOOK

Jack Peters is everything a girl could want in a bad boy. Blunt, aloof, and ready to whisk you away on the back of his motorcycle. And that's just the way he likes it. Simple relationships. No commitment. High adrenaline. A shapeshifting hellhound with a look that kills—literally—Jack hides behind his sunglasses and skulks in the cemeteries, biding his time until he's out of Havenwood Falls and on the road to bigger adventures.

He doesn't plan on Cressida Manos.

A seventeen-year-old mountain nymph, Cressida has it all. A great family. A quiet life. And an annoying habit of being overly helpful and friendly with everyone. She's sunny, cheerful, dependable, and . . . a vandal?

Caught on camera tagging buildings in the middle of the night, no one can believe Cressida Manos capable of malicious destruction of property. Especially Jack Peters, who stumbles on the redhead in the middle of graffitiing a tombstone.

Only Cressida doesn't remember her crimes, and the only one who believes she's innocent is the guy who caught her in the act.

HAVENWOOD FALLS HIGH BOOKS

Written in the Stars by Kallie Ross

Reawakened by Morgan Wylie

The Fall by Kristen Yard

Somewhere Within by Amy Hale

Awaken the Soul by Michele G. Miller

Bound by Shadows by Cameo Renae

Fata Morgana by E.J. Fechenda

Forever Emeline by Katie M. John

Reclamation by AnnaLisa Grant

Avenoir by Daniele Lanzarotta

Avenge the Heart by Michele G. Miller

Curse the Night by R.K. Ryals

Blood & Iron by Amy Hale

Shadows & Spells by Cameo Renae

Falling Deep by J.L. Weil

Saving Infiniti by Rose Garcia

Willful by Liz Ferry

Cast in Moonlight by Ali Winters

Promise the Moon by Kallie Ross

Blurred Lines by Daniele Lanzarotta

Ascending Darkness by J.L. Weil

Finding Infiniti by Rose Garcia

Unicorn's Lament by Megan Linski

Paper Bird by Amy Richie

Predestined by Valia Lind

Rediscovered by Morgan Wylie

Ashes of Fate by Apryl Baker

Stay up to date at <u>www.HavenwoodFalls.com</u>

ALSO BY R.K. RYALS

Fist of the Furor

City in Ruins

The Standalone Embrace Yourself Series

The Story of Awkward

An Introvert's Tale

Contemporary Romance Reads

The Singing River

Hawthorne & Heathcliff

The Best I Could

Sex & Such

Capture the World

CURSE THE NIGHT

A HAVENWOOD FALLS HIGH NOVELLA

R.K. RYALS

For those who find strength in differences and confidence in being yourself.
Let your light shine.

"Walking with a friend in the dark is better than walking alone in the light."
~Helen Keller~

PROLOGUE

JACK PETERS

No matter the time of day, the clubhouse was rarely empty. Unconscious bodies littered the space, the forms sprawled across the floor, the threadbare sofa lining the walls, and the pool table resting in the center of the room. Half-naked women spooned with men in leather vests sporting a sword-impaled skull and patches. Empty beer bottles and specially mixed brews from Sanguine Elixirs dripped sticky liquid onto scarred hardwood floors. Blood, alcohol, and God knew what else.

I snorted. The prospects were going to hate cleaning up the mess.

Club SIN. That was the name I called it in my head. The place where the Swords of the Infernal Night congregated. A motorcycle club on the wrong side *and* the right side of the law. One percenters. And my dad was their leader. I was the prodigal son, the tattooed jackass he hoped would take over for him one day.

Maybe I would.

Picking my way around the bodies, I walked toward a door at the back of the room, my stride full of purpose and determination.

I knew he was in there, and I knew he was awake. He always was.

The door made no sound when I opened it.

Inside the room, a man sat at a long mahogany table, his head bent over a stack of papers, his fingers twirling a knife. I watched it spin on the wood.

"Pops."

Liam Peters looked up, his hard gaze finding mine, the sunglasses he always wore pushed up on top of his head. My father was light where I was dark, his sandy hair a little too long, his face covered in scruff. Tattoos lined his arms. His chest and shoulders were broad, filling out the leather cut he rarely removed. Havenwood Falls' finest nearly untouchable outlaw. He and his business partner, Tychon Savage—or just Savage, as everyone knew him—were the epitome of good and evil. For them, there was no line separating the two. They *were* the line.

"Pops, I need your help."

CHAPTER 1

CRESSIDA MANOS

FIVE DAYS EARLIER . . .

"What is a four-letter word for 'being connected to someone'?" Paris asked, her pencil poised over the page of her open book, the front cover folded under the back. Light poured in through a large picture window overlooking Main Street, the glow highlighting the stained concrete flooring, light yellow walls, and multicolored display cases lining the interior of my family's art business, Apex Art Studio. It was early June in Havenwood Falls, the ease of summer already sinking into the bones, comfortable and unhurried. A peaceful respite before Midsummer's Night Terrors, a festival held in the square on the Summer Solstice.

Wet clay covered my hands, my fingers working the lump on the potter's wheel. I was responsible for the handmade pottery the customers painted—the pieces we didn't have shipped in—and I loved it. The entire creative process was soothing. Hypnotizing.

"Is that the only hint?" I asked, pressing my thumb into the center of the lump, my gaze flicking to the dark-haired, dark-skinned girl sitting cross-legged on the floor next to my stool.

Named after the place where her parents met and where she was

3

conceived, my best friend Paris Francine Callahan was fascinated with crossword puzzles and had been since the day we were introduced in elementary school. Paris was human—an important distinction in Havenwood Falls, where a substantial portion of the population was supernatural—and shy. Extremely shy. Even though she was stunning enough to grace the cover of Vogue. I was the plain one out of the two of us, all five foot one, redheaded, pale-skinned, button-nosed, freckled inch of me.

"One of a matched pair?" Paris added, reading. "Third letter is a T."

"Mate." The word slipped off my tongue too easily.

Paris penciled it in. "It works. How did I miss that?" She glanced up at me. "How did *you* get that?"

I kept my gaze locked on the vase forming before me. Having a mate was common in the supernatural world, depending on the species. I was an oread, a mountain nymph, and while we didn't mate or bond, I knew enough supes who did. As for Paris, she was completely oblivious to Havenwood Falls' supernatural side. If she suspected something was off, she never mentioned it.

There was a rumble down the street, the sound of revving motorcycles getting louder as a group of men in leather vests cruised past our shop window.

Paris set her book aside and hugged her knees. "Do you think they're dangerous?"

I was too close to finishing the vase to look away. "SIN? No doubt."

SIN, or Swords of the Infernal Night, was Havenwood Falls' local motorcycle club. The club kept to itself, which was why it was rarely a topic of conversation in town. It was no secret they existed. They owned a delivery company, Cerberus Delivery Inc., and their trucks were the main means of delivering goods from outside town to businesses and individuals in Havenwood Falls. The sister of the club's vice president also owned Silk, an exclusive nightclub. But no one discussed them or their businesses, especially Silk's private clientele. I knew more than I should, because my father tended to talk too much about work at home. Not only did Cerberus—more commonly referred to as CDI—deliver unique goods to my father's business, but many of Silk's well-off clients liked buying expensive jewelry.

What *was* a secret—to the mortals anyhow—was that the leader of SIN, Liam Peters, and his business partner, Savage, were shapeshifting hellhounds. Most of their club members were supernatural. Maybe even all of them.

"The dangerous part is kind of hot," Paris admitted. "Though I wouldn't want to find out how dangerous," she rushed to add. "It's like wanting to eat an entire plate of chocolate. Tempting, but no."

Paris was diabetic, which played into her reserved nature. Her mother was overly protective, and Paris wasn't fond of testing her blood sugar or giving herself insulin shots in front of people.

"Why, Paris, are you into bad boys?" I teased.

She snorted. "As long as they're more 'rebel without a cause' and not Hannibal Lecter."

Finishing the vase, I glanced at her. "So, you'll warm the bed of a heartbreaker with a rap sheet, but not a serial killer. Noted."

Neither one of us had warmed anyone's bed. We were both going into our senior year at Havenwood Falls High in the fall, and neither of us had even been kissed. Paris was too shy, and I was always friend-zoned.

The studio door opened, and my sister, Leda, walked in, her brows arched. Pulling her key out of the lock, she shook it at us. "Why bolt the door when you have the closed sign up?"

The door being locked wasn't a bad thing, but it annoyed Leda when she had to dig for her keys instead of being able to just walk in.

"We're keeping rapscallions out." I gestured at her. "Case in point."

"Rapscallions?" Leda laughed, her gaze passing between us. "You two say the weirdest things. That word is seventeenth-century old."

"Tell that to Dad."

"Yeah, well, Dad's . . ." Her sentence trailed off, but I knew what she left unsaid. Dad's age predated the word. At six hundred ten years old, he predated a lot of things. "Can you catch the shipment for Apex out back and put out new inventory before we open on Monday?"

"Wasn't that supposed to come in yesterday?" Standing, I rushed to a paint-stained, industrial-sized sink built into the wall at the back of the room. The clay on my hands turned the water tan as it circled the basin to disappear down the drain.

I was a study in disarray, my unruly red hair bunched on top of my head, my body hidden by a light blue button-up shirt, overalls, and an apron. I was the complete opposite of my sister. She was tall where I was short, slender where I was skinny, blonde where I was redheaded, and elegant where I was laidback and disorganized.

Leda's heels clicked on the concrete floor, her red shoes complementing her black dress pants, black suit jacket, and red blouse. Her fingers sparkled. Rings were an everyday fashion accessory for her, and she had easy access to them. Not only did my family own the art studio on Main, but we also owned a jewelry store, Summit Jewelry, on the corner of Eighth and Main, next door. Like my sister and I, the two stores couldn't be any more different. While Apex was a chaotic, colorful shop that smelled like paint, Summit Jewelry was an elegant store with shining hardwood flooring, hanging chandeliers, and a showcase floor full of glass cases.

"Dad got word of a rare jewel he wanted at an auction outside town. He won the bid on it, and CDI was kind enough to wait the extra day to deliver. For an added fee, of course. I've already got the shipment for the jewelry store and locked up Dad's new prize. The jewel is pretty, I'll give him that, but it probably cost us a fortune." Bitter humor colored Leda's voice. "I'm headed back to the store. Make sure they don't break anything."

Tucking my hands into the pockets of my apron, I turned to Paris. "Want to help?"

"SIN is out back? As in now?" Her eyes went wide. Paris worked part time at Apex, but her hours rarely coincided with shipments.

"It *is* their delivery company."

She launched to her feet, instantly towering over me, and touched her hair nervously.

Leading the way, I opened a door at the back of the studio and stepped into a storeroom. Another door led into the alley, and it stood open, no doubt courtesy of my sister.

A boy I instantly recognized but had never met ducked into the space, wheeling a stack of boxes in front of him. He was tall, at least six feet two, and while that was intimidating, it was nothing compared to most hellhounds. He had a lot of room to grow. The white short-sleeve T-shirt stretched across his torso was mostly hidden by a plain leather cut, which meant he wasn't a part of the motorcycle club, but —if the rumors I'd heard were any indication—he also wasn't opposed to it. He was ripped, his muscles straining against the fabric as he unloaded the boxes. A thick chain tattoo wrapped his left arm, starting somewhere beneath his sleeve and circling down to his forearm. Other tattoos I couldn't make out peeked at us from under his right sleeve. Dark hair, cut close to his head but left longer on the top, fell carelessly onto his forehead, bringing attention to the expensive sunglasses covering his eyes.

Paris inhaled sharply behind me, trying desperately to make herself as small as possible, even though I made a terrible shield.

Jack Peters. Middle son of SIN's leader, Liam Peters. Although I didn't *know* him, I recognized him easily. He was seventeen and a rising senior at the prestigious Sun and Moon Academy, and we had a lot of the same acquaintances. I'd say friends, but I wasn't sure he had those. He was as elusive as his father and his father's club.

"Hi," I greeted him cheerfully. Jack didn't respond. I wasn't even sure he looked at me.

"You need help moving this stuff into the store?" a deep, raspy voice asked, and I nearly jumped out of my skin. Paris squeaked.

A man entered, his large body completely stealing whatever oxygen and space was left in the room. This man, *everyone* knew. While I was used to CDI and their deliveries, I'd never actually met the head of the motorcycle club. Sightings of Liam Peters in town didn't count.

Liam surpassed his son by several inches, his massive build filling out a leather cut plastered in patches. Sunglasses shielded his eyes, his chiseled jaw covered in scruff. He wore his sandy blond hair a little long, his obvious tattoos far outnumbering Jack's.

"That'd be good," I managed, backing me and Paris into the studio. Paris's fingers dug painfully through the back of my overalls.

"They're massive," she breathed.

"Shh," I hissed, lightly kicking her.

"Isn't that Jack Peters?" she asked, nodding at the younger man, completely ignoring my attempt to shush her. If only she knew how well hellhounds could hear.

Liam and Jack unloaded boxes along the wall, an awkward silence falling.

"Do you think they kill people who can't make conversation?" Paris mumbled.

I jabbed her with my elbow, and while I didn't have the hearing hellhounds did, I didn't miss Liam's faint chuckle.

Too much time passed, all of it in silence, the sound of boxes thudding the only noise in the room.

"What's takin' so long?" a petulant voice called, followed by feet stomping into the studio.

Now *this* voice I was used to. Cade Peters. The youngest son of Liam, and a literal pain in the rear on a *good* day. He often rode along on deliveries, and he was really good at driving me crazy. Full of confidence, he strutted across the room, his sunglasses resting securely on his nose. I just hoped he didn't remove them. It wouldn't affect me if he did, but it would hurt Paris. If a human or a non-immortal supernatural peered into a hellhound's eyes three times, it was a death sentence. Hence the sunglasses. It was also the reason all the Peters boys attended the Academy rather than Havenwood Falls High.

Cade barely spared me a glance, but he gave Paris his undivided attention. "What's up, Manos? Who's the friend you got there?"

"Nope," I said, nose scrunched. "You can take your fourteen-year-old hormones to someone else's door, Peters."

My words did nothing to deter him. After a wholly appreciative once-over—this would be impossible for anyone else while wearing shades but was somehow completely possible for a Peters—he glanced at my potter's wheel. I slid in front of it, arms crossing. The last time he appreciated my art, I lost two vases and a really awesome unicorn. Kids loved the unicorns. And the dragons.

"Whatcha workin' on there?" he asked, attempting to dodge me. At fourteen, he was already taller than me, but I was quicker. "Ponies and rainbows?"

"Depends. You interested in ponies and rainbows?"

Again with the Liam chuckle.

Cade scowled. "The only thing I like to ride, Manos, is—"

"Cade," Liam warned, the rumble of his voice enough to make both Paris and me jump. "What have I told you about respecting ladies?"

"Really, Pops, that ain't no lady, that's just Cress—"

Jack popped him on the back of the head, having come up behind him too quick for any of us to see. When Cade tried to protest, Jack popped him again.

"*Isn't* a lady," he corrected. "And be glad it wasn't Pops." His voice was as deep and raspy as his father's.

"Sorry, ladies," Liam said, finishing up with the boxes. "He hears crap from the boys and thinks it's okay to repeat it. He doesn't have the best examples at home. Least of all a motherly one."

"Melaina—" Cade began.

"My point exactly," Liam mumbled, cutting him off. "Excuse us, ladies."

I followed them to the storeroom, pausing at the door to the alley. Jack lingered, stopping just short of walking out the door.

"You've got . . . stuff," he touched my cheek lightly, the heat of his fingers startling me, "here." He dropped his hand as fast as he lifted it, and I hated that I couldn't see his eyes.

"Oh." I touched the spot, my fingers brushing over dried clay. "Thank you."

He left, climbing on a motorcycle in the alley. Liam straddled a Harley nearby. Cade hopped into the passenger side of a delivery truck, a burly man in a CDI uniform peering out at me from the driver's seat.

"Your dad has some expensive taste in jewelry," Liam told me, pulling on a helmet. "That was a nice rock we dropped off at Summit. Tell him if he needs another *special* delivery, to let us know. I told your sister the same thing, but you look like you may be better at delivering messages."

"Leda isn't a huge fan of Dad's odd tastes in antiques," I admitted. Leda wasn't a fan of the *money* she knew Dad spent on things that fascinated him, and Dad had a very large collection of things that fascinated him, everything from vintage watches to Persian rugs.

"I gathered that," Liam replied, flashing me a knowing grin.

His motorcycle revved, and they were off, the bikes escorting the delivery truck down the street. My fingers brushed my cheek. I could still feel the heat of Jack's touch, and it unsettled me. Were all hellhounds that warm?

Closing the door to the alley, I locked it and reentered the studio.

"That was exciting!" Paris called, her voice echoing from a small restroom near the utility sink, the door cracked.

"You missed them leaving," I told her.

"I had to pee. You know I always have to pee when I get nervous." The toilet flushed, and the sink turned on.

I dug through a desk drawer at the front of the studio.

"They weren't anything like I thought they'd be." Paris exited the bathroom. "Except the youngest, which is weird."

Box cutter in hand, I went for the boxes. It was going to be a long afternoon, but it was the first Saturday in months we didn't have paint-and-sip reservations. Or a birthday party, for that matter. Which made it perfect for doing inventory.

Paris went for the price gun. "All those rumors about Jack Peters— do you think they're true?"

If only she knew. Havenwood Falls was full of rumors, and most of the time when it came to the supernaturals, if it wasn't the truth, it was close enough. Jack's reputation preceded him, and while it wasn't as bad as his father's, his was certainly headed in the same direction. It would scare any sensible person away. He was the kind of guy girls snuck out to spend a night with just so they could say they did, the kind of guy other guys hit up for favors they knew no one else would do, and the kind of guy who had no problem crossing lines.

He was the kind of guy a girl should stay far, far away from.

"Yeah, I think most of them are true," I replied. Pulling ceramic figurines out of the first box, I set them aside, then collapsed the cardboard. My cheek still burned, and I swiped at it.

"What are you . . ." Paris began, then leaned toward me. "I think you may have gotten yourself with your fingernail or something. There's a pink spot on your face."

I stared at her. "What?"

"It's barely noticeable. I wouldn't have seen it if you didn't keep rubbing at it."

"Do you have your phone?" I asked. I had a cell, but I rarely carried it on me. The service was so bad in Havenwood Falls, it was practically pointless.

Paris dug a phone out of her blue jeans pocket and handed it to me. I clicked on her camera icon, using the self-image feature to look at my face. There, on the bridge of my cheek, was a tiny pink spot, smaller than any of my freckles. A very small burn.

"Really, I can hardly see it," Paris assured me.

It wasn't the pink spot that bothered me. It was knowing how it got there in the first place. Jack Peters had *burned* me.

I probed it carefully before returning Paris's phone. "Guess I did get myself somehow. It'll go away."

Returning to the boxes, I cut a new one open, my thoughts scattered. I wasn't sure what disturbed me more—the burn, or the little part of me that didn't want the burn to heal.

CHAPTER 2

JACK PETERS

The best part of riding my motorcycle was the wind. The vibration of the bike and the freedom were part of the euphoria, too, but it was the wind that made me feel like I was flying. As if I could shut my eyes and suddenly take off into the air. As if I could escape who and what I was. Not that I hated being me. Out of all of Liam's sons, I was the one most like my father, which was exciting and terrifying.

"You're super droll today," Cade called out after we'd pulled into the delivery company's parking lot and switched off our engines. My fourteen-year-old brother jumped out of the passenger seat of the truck, a goofy grin plastered on his face.

I pushed the kickstand down on my bike. "Droll?"

"I heard it from Cressida. The chick from the art store."

Our father, Liam Peters, sauntered toward us, and even though his eyes were hidden by his sunglasses, I knew he was amused. "The pixie?"

"She's an oread, a mountain nymph, Pops," Cade huffed. "She's expanding my vocabulary."

Liam snorted. "Then learn how to use it correctly, son. Otherwise you just sound stupid."

I laughed. "Is that what was happening today? You were getting an education?"

Liam removed his fingerless riding gloves and slapped them against his jeans. "If you've got a crush on that redhead, I need to teach you better flirting skills."

"Whatever." Cade started to brush past us, the heat pouring off his skin nearly scalding.

Face hard, Pops took Cade by the shoulder, stopping him. "Girls aside, you've got to get a better grip on your emotions. If someone were to touch you right now, they'd get burned. Jack isn't droll; he's calm." With his free hand, Pops pulled his sunglasses down the bridge of his nose, his red-tinted eyes peering at Cade over the brim. "You can't play with romance if you have to worry about killing someone."

"Romance?" I chuckled, because I knew doing anything else would only embarrass Cade further. Pops wasn't subtle. He treated his sons like members of the club rather than his children. "The nymph is too old for you."

Cade pouted. "By three years. Age is just a number."

Climbing off my bike, I slapped my brother on the back. "Cressida Manos doesn't date."

"What?" Cade's features relaxed, his skin cooling. "Where'd you hear that?"

I honestly couldn't remember where I'd first heard the nymph wasn't into dating, but it was common knowledge among our graduating class, both at Havenwood Falls High and Sun and Moon Academy. It was also common knowledge that her older sister, Leda, was into girls. Considering Cressida's dateless high school record, it was assumed she was, too. But judging from the startled look she'd given me when I brushed the clay off her cheek at the studio, I was beginning to doubt that.

The memory brought a smile to my lips. I was used to the way girls reacted around me, both the shy girls and the flirtatious ones, but Cressida hadn't come on to me. She'd reacted to the touch, a blush riding high on her cheeks, her green eyes wide and unnerved. Up until that moment, she'd been too focused on keeping her friend's voice down and my snarky brother in line to pay me any attention. Maybe that's why I'd let my guard down, singeing her face. Thing is, I didn't know why I'd done it, and Pops would have killed me if he knew.

Cade threw me a disgruntled look. "She just needs the right guy. You wait and see—I'll wear her down."

"More like scare her off," I mumbled as my brother trotted off, determination etching his brows. Ah, the joys of crushing on someone. I hated what the future held for him. Girls didn't want romance from guys like us. They wanted a good time and a good story to go with it.

"You've got to stop comparing us," I told Pops when Cade disappeared into the clubhouse across from the delivery company. "I read in some magazine that comparing your children only causes dissent and mistrust."

Liam pulled his sunglasses off. "When did you start reading parenting magazines?"

"I was looking for an article about an archeological dig in South America. The parenting shit was just in there."

"And you read it?'

My lips twitched, and I grimaced in an attempt not to smile. "Someone has to. It wouldn't hurt for you to check that stuff out every once in a while, Pops."

He smacked me on the back of the head, hard enough to get my attention but soft enough I knew he did it out of affection. "I'm trying to make you boys tough. The world doesn't work like those articles."

"Maybe not, but could you use Savage as your example next time? Dealing with Cade's sulking is enough to give me indigestion." Savage was Pops's best friend, his business partner, the vice president of SIN, and a fellow hellhound. He'd always been a part of our lives, enough like family we'd called him uncle as children. Which was why using him as an example of an "exemplary hellhound" would be a lot better than telling Cade he needed to act like me. Cade respected Savage. He resented me.

Liam rubbed the bridge of his nose. "How'd you end up so much like your mother?"

"Luck."

Pops smacked me on the back of the head again, and I backed away, laughing.

"Your mother would have made a damn fine club president if she'd been born male."

"Is that a hint, Pops?"

Liam cocked his brows. "Just a suggestion, son. You know Taemin isn't cut out for the life. Your older brother is better suited for hacking computers than he is running a motorcycle club, and Cade is way too hotheaded."

"I'll keep that in mind."

Pops and I were good at this game. He knew how to get under my skin, and I was becoming a pro at evading his expectations. Scary thing was, I knew I'd like running the MC because, as much as I pretended I wasn't like my father, there was one thing we had in common: for us, being in power felt good.

CHAPTER 3

CRESSIDA MANOS

$\mathcal{M}$onday came too quick, my cat's fluffy tail hitting me in the face minutes before my alarm went off. Kittypatra McSlinky, Slink for short, was a needy pet, especially in the morning. Her way of garnering attention included countless minutes nibbling my toes under the comforter, followed by wagging her butt in my face.

I shoved her aside gently. Oreads didn't require much sleep, but that didn't mean I didn't like sleeping.

Slink pawed at me, and I ruffled the hair between her ears. The tortoise-hair cat wasn't just my pet; she was my responsibility. I was the only one in the house who liked her. Mom was of the "your cat, your problem" mentality. Dad referred to her as "that damn cat" because she had a thing for clawing his expensive suits when he left them hanging in the laundry room. Before Leda moved out, she and the feline spent every morning in a hissing match because Slink liked peeing in Leda's brand-name shoes.

"You're just misunderstood, aren't you, you little cutie?" Slink rolled over, and I ran my fingers down her soft belly, her purr vibrating against my palm.

Mom and Dad were already gone when I finally made it downstairs, my hair clipped up and my trusty, worn cut-off shorts paired with an equally worn sweatshirt. Even though it wasn't sweatshirt weather—temps generally averaged in the upper seventies in Colorado in June—I didn't feel cold or heat the same way most people did. I wore the sweatshirts and oversized clothes so I didn't have to wear a bra, the upside to being flat-chested. The people in town assumed I was cold-natured. The key to fitting in with humans was maintaining a consistent image. And I hated bras.

After dumping cat food in a bowl by the refrigerator, I grabbed a granola bar from the pantry, slipped my feet into a pair of polka-dotted red rain boots, and hurried out the door. The morning was misty, the cool wetness like gentle tears on my cheeks. Even clipped up, I could feel my hair frizz. As an oread, traveling by foot was quicker than standard human transportation, especially in the mountains where our house was located, just far enough from town to feel at home among the rocks. Oreads could jump impossible distances, fall from crazy heights, and run extremely fast. We were like Olympic high-jumpers on steroids. My parents owned a car, because not having one when we lived out of town would look suspicious, but we didn't need one.

Running, I eyed a drop-off in the distance, dodging trees and foliage as I sped toward it. Lungs filling with sweet, damp air, I jumped over the side of the cliff, laughing as I fell. The wind pounded me in my face, my toes curling to keep my boots from falling off. I landed hard—hard enough to kill a human—but my feet and body absorbed the impact like a sponge. Mom would kill me if she saw me, but my favorite part of being an oread was the falling. Most people feared falling, but I lived for the exhilaration of it. I lived for the freedom.

Breathing hard, I crouched, laughter rolling out of me, the sound echoing through the mountains. The laugh bounced back at me so clearly, it was as if it came from someone else, as if I was laughing with a friend rather than alone. An oread could echo her voice from anywhere. It made having an imaginary friend as a child so much easier. I'd spent hours talking to myself as a kid, asking questions and then echoing back a reply.

My laughter still ringing on the breeze, I broke into a run, the world blurring past me. At the edge of town, I slowed, carefully making my way down the back roads until I reached the south side of town, where Tenth Street intersected with Petran Road. A large parking lot full of eighteen-wheeler trucks and two large buildings loomed on one side of the street. The building closer to the trucks was a massive, metal warehouse with a loading dock at the back. Double glass doors on the front were etched with the figure of a three-headed, ferocious hound. Cerberus Delivery, Inc.

Motorcycles lined the building opposite the warehouse. This building was smaller, the exterior redbrick with a thick wooden door, the SIN logo hanging above it. The sword-impaled skull stared back at me, and I found myself fascinated with the image. As if it could see things in me I couldn't quite understand. Maybe it could.

The door to the building flew open, and Cade Peters marched out, his expression sour. I groaned inwardly. I passed the CDI warehouse and the SIN clubhouse every time I volunteered at the local animal shelter, but it was always too early for me to run into anyone. We Manoses were early birds.

"Come on! It's summer, Pops!" Cade roared.

Two women followed him out the door, each of them with mussed hair, hastily pulled-on clothes, dangling purses, and smeared lipstick.

"Better not to argue, honey," one of the ladies said, her hand vanishing into her purse. A cigarette appeared in her fingers, and she stuck it between her lips before drawing out a lighter.

Men in leather cuts, all of them too large for their own good, stumbled out after the women, all of them grumbling.

"It's too early for this shit," one of them said before climbing onto a motorcycle. He pulled a helmet off the handlebars and shoved it onto his head.

"Should have laid off the liquor," a familiar deep voice replied, amused. Jack Peters ambled over to his brother, gravel crunching beneath his combat boots, while he pulled his leather cut on over a plain white T-shirt.

"Tell your dad he's supposed to let us know this shit beforehand, so we can," the guy groused.

Jack laughed, the deep rumble so beautiful, the air drank it appreciatively. No one should look or sound that good. It was a crime against humanity. "Pops likes catching people off guard."

Cade glanced up, his gaze passing over me, and I stumbled forward, pulse quickening. *Not today, Peters. Please not today.*

"Yo, Manos!" Cade shouted. He ran toward me, and if I wasn't so worried about the mortals in Havenwood Falls, I'd have taken off like lightning. "I thought I smelled coconut."

Spinning, I smiled brightly, because no matter how irritating and moody he could be, I still liked Cade. "You're up early."

His black hair caught the sun, the rays tinting it blue in the light. Cade was a contradiction. Taller and broader than humans and most supernaturals, he was still shorter and lankier than typical hellhounds. I knew this because my dad spent a good deal of time drilling my sister and me about supernatural creatures. As we were my parents' only children, Dad was hell-bent on making sure we knew how to protect ourselves from anything.

"Why? Do you pass here often?" Cade asked, a grin splitting his face.

Why couldn't I keep my mouth shut? "Nope," I answered too quickly, the lie obvious. I was terrible at lying.

Cade perused my figure, and I was suddenly glad the Peterses all wore sunglasses. I wasn't sure what it was Cade saw in me. Most of the time I couldn't figure out if he was giving me a tough time or if he had a crush. A tough time made way more sense than the crush thing. I wasn't anything like the type of girl the Peters men hung out with.

"You headed to the studio?" Cade asked, sinking his hands into his blue jeans pockets, his shoulders hunching up to his ears even though it wasn't cold outside.

"What's with the getup?" Jack Peters sidled up next to Cade, his presence swallowing his younger brother's. Because of their size, hellhounds appeared older than their actual ages. Up until a certain point. Once they reached adulthood, however, they seemed to quit aging.

My reflection stared back at me in his sunglasses, and my cheeks heated. "It's comfy couture. You should try it. It's all the rage in summer."

Jack glanced down. "And the rain boots?"

"We're going to get showers today." Oreads were also good at predicting the weather.

In unison, the brothers glanced at the sky. Blue. No clouds.

I grinned. "Mid-afternoon, right after lunch."

"Really?" Cade whistled. "You're full of surprises, Manos."

"It's nothing special," I said, shrugging. "My parents and sister can do it, too. They're better at it."

"Does it ever hurt?" Jack asked suddenly, genuinely.

My gaze flew to his face. "What?"

"Smiling like that. Every time I see you around town, you're grinning."

"That's just Cressy," Cade reassured.

"Cressida," I corrected. I hated, hated, *hated* it when people shortened my name.

"Cress," Cade teased.

"Cressida." Still smiling, I shook my fist at him.

Cade pulled down his sunglasses, a mischievous glint in his red-hued eyes. "Ressy . . . Ida . . . Sid."

It was taking everything I had not to hit him.

"Put your sunglasses back on," Jack demanded, the command sobering the mood.

Cade glared at him. "It doesn't affect oreads."

"That doesn't mean you should take them off." Reaching out, Jack replaced his brother's sunglasses. "You'll get in the habit of removing them."

"God, you sound like Pops," Cade mumbled.

They were kind of cute when they argued, sort of like puppies yipping at each other. "You guys." Stuffing myself between them, I took them each by the arm. "Haven't you ever heard that fighting before breakfast is really bad for digestion?"

Cade and Jack froze, and the moment grew uncomfortable. They had biceps of freaking steel. It was like being wedged between two walls.

"Is she for real?" Jack whispered over my head.

Cade shrugged, dislodging my hand. "Maybe she didn't get the memo." He glanced down at me. "Girls don't touch Jack."

"What?" That had to be the most ridiculous thing I'd ever heard. Especially considering the number of ex-lovers he had in town. I laughed and made it a point to pat Jack's arm. "That's not what I hear."

Slowly and deliberately, Jack carefully peeled my fingers away from him. "You need permission first."

His skin suddenly warmed, and I yanked my hand away, cradling it. "Hey, now!" My fingers stung.

Cade's mouth fell open. "Did you just burn her? Like, seriously?"

Sticking a few of my fingers in my mouth, I sucked on them. "What was that for? That hurt!"

"Seriously," Cade barked out a harsh laugh, "after all of the lectures from you and Pops about controlling this and controlling that, and you go and burn someone."

Jack took a step back, creases forming between his eyebrows. "I—"

"What's with the commotion out here?" Liam Peters appeared behind his sons.

I stuffed my hand behind my back, so quickly I'm sure it looked more awkward and telling than genuine.

Cade nodded at his brother. "Pops, Jack—"

"Was just telling me that he doesn't think it's going to rain today, but it's definitely going to happen." Words spilled out of me, so fast they ran into each other. "likereallygoingtohappenandit'sgoingto"—I took a deep breath—"you know, rain."

Liam's gaze dropped to my arm, and I tucked my hand farther behind my back. Damn hellhounds and their ultra-heightened senses.

"Is that so?" Liam asked, his mouth tightening. "You would know, right?" He nudged his son, and I couldn't help but wonder what his eyes looked like right now. If his voice was any indication, Liam was angry, and he was having a challenging time holding it in. "Listen to the oread, son. They know a thing or two about the weather."

I started backing toward the road. "Hence the rain boots." Nervous laughter escaped me. "They're really good for puddle jumping." My mouth needed to close now. Like, really.

Jack snorted. "What are you? Twelve?"

I couldn't tell if he was playing along because he didn't want to admit he'd burned my hand, or if he was really being sarcastic. I chose to believe he was playing along.

Tapping my chest with my non-throbbing hand, I flashed a smile at the group. "In my heart, I am. Gotta go! I'm late!"

Without a single glance backward, I hightailed it to the end of Petran Road, heart pounding. My breathing was labored when I finally stopped, not from exhaustion but from nervous excitement. In the distance, Danzan Park spread out before me, the large grounds on the southeast corner of town and near my destination. At several hundred acres, Danzan Park was a place full of countless fun outdoor opportunities. There was a playground, a picnic area, dog park, disc golf course, public pool, soccer fields, basketball courses, ice rink, skate park, and a spacious area for concerts and festivals. There was also a lake. I spent a lot of time walking dogs there.

Lifting my wounded hand, I studied it. Despite the redness of my fingers, the burns didn't hurt anymore. The spots weren't bad enough to blister, but they should have felt more uncomfortable than they did. Adrenaline, maybe? Some weird hellhound pain-numbing magic? Or had Jack only meant to scare me?

"You're later than usual," a female voice called out.

Dogs of all shapes and sizes jumped up on a chain-link fence, tails wagging and tongues lolling. Some of them raced around the pen barking while others rested in the grass.

Isa Hilton, Havenwood Falls' resident veterinarian, approached me from the side of a nondescript stone building. A sign hanging from a post in the yard read *Havenwood Falls Animal Shelter.* I had volunteered at the shelter for a couple of years, even fostering Slink before deciding to adopt her. While I didn't get the chance to volunteer as much as I had in the past, I made it a point to come once a week.

A much nicer building close to the shelter had a manicured lawn and paw-shaped stepping stones leading up to a shining glass door. A sign near the road read *Havenwood Falls Animal Hospital.* Both buildings were owned and operated by Isa. Isa was the most interesting human I'd ever met. With dark hair and wide-set eyes, she was beautiful, her features a strong testament to her mother's Korean roots. Her height, she once told me, came from her father.

A tattoo, a yellow sunflower wrapped by a thorny black rose, peeked out at me from her wrist, her white lab coat obscuring most of the design. The tattoo was Court-issued. All the supernatural creatures in Havenwood Falls were required to have one—mine was a charm bracelet tattooed around my ankle—which was why Isa was so fascinating. Although she was human, she had telekinetic powers. *Strong* telekinetic powers.

"The kittens in the back need worming." Isa paused in front of me, a pen poised over a day planner in her hand. "We had an unexpected drop-off last night—two beagle mixes that need dipping. Other than that, it's just the basic duties."

I scrunched my nose. "None of the other volunteers came in this morning, did they?"

Isa sighed. "It's so much harder to find good volunteers during the summer. Why is that?"

"Vacations, sleep, parties, hookups, more sleep . . . geez, I have no idea what the allure could be. I much prefer cleaning up dog poo and worming baby kittens."

Isa shook her pen at me, her megawatt smile revealing a dimple in her cheek. "Sad thing is, you actually mean that when you *should* be doing all that other stuff, except maybe not the hooking up."

"Well, I guess you don't need the extra help th—"

Jerking me toward the shelter, Isa whopped me on the rear with her day planner. "Go. Scoot. I won't say another word."

Chuckling, I walked into the building, my nose taken hostage by the overwhelming odor of bleach and flea control products. Opening cabinets in the cramped back room, I found the kitten wormer, made my way to the cat room, and got to work.

It was after lunch when the rain began, the sound soft on the shelter's roof. Because I'd known it was coming, I'd retrieved the dogs from the outside pen and was leaning against the wall, listening to it pelting the windows, when the uneasiness suddenly hit me. A dark, strange sensation, sharp and painful, bloomed in my stomach, and I doubled over, my head spinning. As quickly as it appeared, the pain and dizziness left me, but the uneasiness remained.

"What?" I mumbled, clutching my abdomen. For most, occasional pain and lightheadedness were a normal part of life, stemming from a host of causes, from malnutrition or disease to a menstrual cycle.

But I wasn't most people, and I certainly wasn't normal.

Oreads didn't get sick. Not ever. We could get injured, but we did *not* get sick. If we died, it was because someone or something deliberately killed us. Which meant whatever had happened to me wasn't remotely close to normal for my kind.

"Hey, you okay?" Isa walked in, snapping an umbrella shut behind her.

I straightened, startled. "Yeah . . ." I shook my head, clearing it. "I just . . ." Just what? "You know, I don't know." Forced laughter leaked out of me. "I'm good." A cold sweat broke out on my brow and, for a moment, I forgot where I was and who I was with. "What did you ask me?"

Isa blinked. "I asked if you were okay."

What did she mean, was I okay? *Something* had just happened, but for the life of me, I couldn't remember what it was. Had I been in pain?

I laughed softly. Whatever. Oreads didn't get sick. "Why wouldn't I be?"

"You were doubled over just now," Isa said gently. "Are you sure you're okay?"

Doubled over? "No . . . I wasn't." Was I? "Everything's good," I promised.

Isa studied me, her dark eyes searching my face, unconvinced. "Okay, I'll take your word for it. We have a mange case boarding at the clinic. I have him isolated, but we're going to need to replace some things after he's back at home. We need to be extra vigilant about washing our hands, so it doesn't spread to the shelter."

"Okay." My thoughts strayed, Isa's words droning on in the background, as comfortable against my ears as the rain pattering against the windows.

Was I okay?

CHAPTER 4

JACK PETERS

"*W*hat the hell were you thinking?*"

Pops's voice rang through my head as I drove my bike through the night. The sun had set hours ago, and although most teens would have had to check in with their parents by now, things worked differently at my house. For one thing, we lived at the MC clubhouse, a place of excess and sin on a difficult day and money and underhanded business deals on a good one. Once I proved I could control my hellhound-given powers, Pops quit keeping tabs on me. Having no rules was supposed to teach me how to get around the law. My recent mess-up hadn't left Pops in the best of moods.

Cressida's shocked face haunted me, her disbelieving look mingling with Pops's angry words in my head. Still, she hadn't ratted me out. Even after she realized Pops knew what happened, his heightened hearing having caught our exchange, she hadn't ratted me out. She'd protected me. That meant a lot to guys like me.

Why did I burn her?

Pulling my motorcycle to a stop outside Havenwood Falls Cemetery, I cut the engine and stared off into the night. Even with my sunglasses on, I could see everything in the dark. A hellhound's heightened senses included night vision. We also didn't sleep much, and if we did, we preferred sleeping during the day.

The cemetery loomed before me, its arched entryway covered in climbing white roses and draped in white wisteria. Water dripped in places from the afternoon rain showers, the *drip-drip* loud in the stillness. Most visitors found the place lonely and sad, but for me, cemeteries felt like home, welcoming and full of love. A place where souls passed through. A place of goodbyes and new beginnings. There *were* hints of anger and loneliness, too, but mostly it was a place of beautiful memories, the serious stuff having been left outside the cemetery grounds. Most souls didn't take bad memories with them in death. In some cases, they forgot their past lives entirely, their spirits prepared for the crossing over. The souls that did take the past with them had some serious anger issues. Either that, or they'd been through some deep shit in life.

Climbing off my bike, I crouched inside the cemetery's entrance, my fingers digging through the damp soil, knuckle deep. Overwhelming warmth flowed through me, calming my troubling thoughts. Cemetery grounds were watered in tears. Grief was one of the strongest forms of love, a release of love so uninhibited, so unrestrained that it was refreshing. I'd cried when my mother passed away, every tear a drop full of the overwhelming affection I'd felt for her.

"Do you know how weird you look when you do that? Especially from the sky."

I didn't look up. I didn't have to. Breckin Roberts and I tended to run into each other often at night. As a Nephilim, part angel and part human, he liked flying when the world was asleep. At six feet two, the recently graduated senior and I were eye to eye, his golden brown hair and amber eyes completely opposite from my soot-colored hair and red-tinted irises. But we had a lot in common. Both of us kept to ourselves, more aloof than social.

Breckin leaned against the cemetery's entryway. "Something's troubling you."

I glanced at him, a small smile playing on my lips. "How are you and Viv these days?"

Vivienne Freeman was Breckin's soul mate, and there'd been a lot of adventure in their lives recently.

Breckin studied me. "Your changing the subject is only making me more curious."

Rising to my feet, I faced him, all pretenses gone. "You and Viv were at Havenwood Falls High. What do you know about Cressida Manos?"

Whatever Breckin expected me to say, it wasn't that. "The mountain nymph?" He stepped away from the entryway. "Red hair. Overly cheerful. Yea high." He lowered his hand, holding it about a foot below his chin. "Little bitty thing."

"That'd be her."

Breckin chuckled. "So *not* your type, man. She's too . . . well behaved. And sweet enough to give anyone a cavity. Seriously, the ultimate optimist. What's up with that?"

"My brother has—"

"No excuses."

"Damn you, Breckin." Grimacing, I ran a hand through my hair. "I burned her. Twice."

Breckin froze. "You what?"

"I burned her."

Silence fell between us, Breckin's incredulous stare making my skin crawl. Being what he was, he knew more than most about how hellhounds worked and the personal rules we liked to follow. A rogue hellhound with no respect for humanity was dangerous.

"You're serious," he said finally, a chuckle escaping with the words.

"It's not funny, man."

"Oh, no, yeah it is. For you to falter like that . . ." He laughed harder. "Cressida Manos, Havenwood Falls High's most likely to be everyone's friend. Damn, I wasn't expecting that."

I glared. "That's what's bugging me. I don't even know her, so I can't figure out why she's getting under my skin. She didn't even do anything."

Breckin started to speak, but I stopped him. "Hellhounds don't do the whole bonding, mating, soul mate thing, so don't even suggest it."

He knew we didn't, but somehow, I felt like it needed to be emphasized. Especially since he was currently glowing with soul mate love.

Breckin shrugged. "Maybe you just like her."

"I don't know her."

"Attracted to her?"

"Have you seen her?"

"That's harsh, dude." Breckin's brows furrowed. "But I see your point. She dresses like she just got out of bed and has no seductive qualities at all. Don't you hellhounds prefer femmes fatales?"

"I don't think this is attraction."

"Don't you only burn when you're angry?"

"That's my point. Something's off."

Breckin grimaced. "I don't think I'm going to be much help tonight, buddy. I'm out, but if you need—"

I waved him off. "Yeah, yeah."

He grinned, backing up before lifting into the sky. I looked away, my gaze dropping to the ground. I knew better than to watch him take flight. With my vision, an angel's wings were bright enough to temporarily blind me.

Talking with Breckin always helped organize my thoughts. Burning Cressida shouldn't have happened, not unless something about her was off somehow. Which begged the question: what was wrong with her?

CHAPTER 5

CRESSIDA MANOS

"*H*ave you been to the jewelry store today?" Mom asked when I entered the house later that night.

Kicking off my rain boots, I inhaled the scent of pizza, a special kind only Mom made with sautéed cashews and water chestnuts on a bed of spinach and grated parmesan and provolone cheese, all of it placed carefully on flatbread and spread with a secret sauce, the ingredients of which Mom refused to divulge. It might sound funny, but my mother's food somehow tasted like the mountains. Like fresh wind blowing down into a ravine or a chilly rain on stone.

"I volunteered at the shelter all day, since you were at the studio. Was I supposed to stop by the store?"

Mom stepped into the foyer, a spoon in her hand. She tasted the sauce on the end, and then offered it to me. "Too salty?"

Barefoot, her auburn hair pulled back from her unlined face, my mother, Theia Manos, looked more like my older sister than my six-hundred-year-old mother.

Licking the spoon, the wonderful flavor exploding on my tongue, I shook my head. "Just right. Don't do a thing to it."

Mom smiled. "Just what I hoped to hear." She reentered the kitchen, banging cabinets open in her haste to finish dinner. "Don't worry about the store. I just wondered if you'd seen the new jewel your dad bid on."

Slink's furry body curled around my ankles as I walked into the kitchen. Full of stainless steel appliances, whitewashed cabinets, and lots of greenery, both fake and real, the kitchen was my mother's favorite place to be. The entire back wall was a display case full of pottery and art projects shoved among rock collections and hanging ferns. Greenhouse-inspired. Magazines would eat it up.

"The one CDI delivered this weekend?" I asked, hopping onto a wrought iron barstool. I'd been in charge of the Apex shipments, but Leda and Liam had both mentioned a special jewel delivery. Dad got a lot of special deliveries.

"That's it. You should see it." Mom's gaze went distant, her blue eyes sparkling. "It's mesmerizing." She peered at me. "It reminds me of your eyes, actually."

"So it's an emerald?"

If there was one thing mountain nymphs loved more than rocks and art, it was precious stones. Anything that came from the earth called to us. We understood stones much better than we understood people. And yet, we were people persons. Go figure.

"Like no emerald I've ever seen. For once, I can't fault your father for this purchase."

I laughed. "What about Leda? Is she giving him a tough time?"

"No, not after seeing it. I think she's just as mesmerized as the rest of us. Speaking of, I think Leda may have a girlfriend. She's been a little off lately. Primping more than usual. Gone longer than normal on her lunch breaks."

"That's great, right?"

Mom set a bowl of sauce on the bar, and I dunked my finger into it. She swatted me with her spoon.

"Maybe. You never know, especially with new relationships. No more sauce until . . ." Mom's words trailed off, her eyes narrowing. "What happened to your fingers?"

I snatched my hand away, shoving it under my leg. "Nothing. A little red paint I couldn't wash off." The burn I'd gotten from Jack was still there, less red but unhealed. Oreads could survive falls and heavy blasts and could heal decently fast when our skin was punctured. Not as fast as some immortals, but decent. But Jack's burn was lingering longer than usual. Maybe because he was a hellhound?

"That didn't look like paint."

"You don't trust me?"

Mom blew out a breath. "That is the worst thing ever a child can ask a parent."

I grinned. "Why?"

"You know why."

My laughter filled the kitchen, echoing off the cabinets. "Seriously, it's all good."

The front door opened, and Dad walked in, his wiry five-foot-nine-inch frame and shocking white blond hair filling the space with a brightness only Dad could manage.

Hanging his suit jacket up by the door, he loosened his tie, then tousled my hair. "What did I miss?"

"Your daughter being petulant." Mom opened the oven and shoved the pizza inside. "You've got twenty minutes until I pull this out."

Dad gave Mom a quick kiss, then rushed up the stairs to change clothes. I sat back, watching Mom as she patted her flushed cheeks, her gaze on his retreating back. I envied their relationship. It was such a beautiful love, over four hundred years strong, the kind I hoped to find someday.

Dad returned in an old sweat suit Mom and I were forever trying to get him to throw away. It was so old, it had holes in places that definitely shouldn't have holes.

"Did you bring the stone home?" Mom asked, retrieving the pizza before setting it on the table.

I moved to the dining room, settling into a seat on the right side of the table while Dad took the head.

"I left it at the store. I feel like it's safer there."

Safer?

Mom tucked the dress she wore under her legs and sat down, her mouth falling open. Dad liked showing off the things he bought. In some cases, we endured hours-long history lessons before being forced to weigh the jewelry in our hands while looking at it from every possible angle.

"Are you worried about theft? Here?" Mom asked.

Dad's brows furrowed. At six hundred ten years old, Dad normally didn't look a day over forty, but tonight he looked older somehow. Troubled. "It's just a feeling."

Mom studied him, frustration evident in her gaze. "Better safe than sorry, I guess. Maybe tomorrow?"

Dad glanced at her, a suspicious glint in his eyes. "Tomorrow? To the house? Why?"

"Why not?" Mom asked.

"You can come by the store to see it."

Our heads shot up, my gaze clinking with Mom's, like two wineglasses before a toast. An awkward, very bad toast. Dad was treating Mom like a customer. A nosy, not appreciated customer.

"I know, but—" Mom began.

"Come there," Dad said firmly and loudly, startling us both. Dad rarely got agitated, and he never raised his voice.

"Okay," Mom replied meekly. "I didn't mean anything by it."

My stomach churned. "If you'll excuse me." Pushing my chair back from the table, I looked at them both. "I think I'm done. It was great, Mom." Truthfully, I'd not even touched the food, my appetite spoiled by their dissent.

My parents barely spared me a glance, their gazes locked on each other. Clutching my stomach, I sped up the stairs, Slink on my heels. My parents weren't the type to argue, and when they did, it wasn't over something as small as a jewel. After four hundred years together, they could read the mood too easily to fight over small things.

"What was that about?" I asked aloud, shedding the clothes I'd worn at the shelter only to replace them with another sweatshirt and a pair of cotton shorts. In the bathroom next to my bedroom, I splashed my face with water, brushed my teeth, and then crawled into my bed.

For some reason, my body felt heavy. Not so much tired as burdened. As if I was trying to pull myself out of quicksand.

Something was off.

My fingers suddenly burned, and I looked down at them warily. Had Jack Peters realized the same thing?

CHAPTER 6

JACK PETERS

A few hours before dawn, I pulled my motorcycle back up to the cemetery. I'd made three trips around town, keeping to the back roads before looping back to the gate, my thoughts a chaotic mess of questions I couldn't answer.

But I knew someone who could.

Cutting off the engine on my bike, I relaxed on the seat, my body beginning to adjust to the silence when the hairs on the back of my neck suddenly stood on end, my eyes, ears, and nose alert to something out of place in the graveyard.

Hellhounds were natural protectors of the dead, of passing souls and those seeking entry into the underworld. While I'd been trained to deal with the dead, and had been forced to on occasion, I'd never had to deal with living trespassers in the Havenwood Falls cemetery. Visitors came in and out at all hours of the night—especially the vampires—but the feeling I got now wasn't coming from a visitor. It was from an intruder, and he was desecrating something. The dead didn't like their graves messed with.

With silent footfalls, I followed a path through the human cemetery to an arched tunnel that went under Blackstone Road, the passageway leading into an older section of the cemetery reserved for Havenwood Falls' supernatural families. This part of the property was a hodgepodge of different tombs. Some of them were protected by metal cages to keep the dead from rising. Others were covered in runes and magic symbols. Mausoleums dotted the front section, and glass balls and crystals hung from the trees, some of them clinking together in the night. Wind chimes—a recent addition by relatives of the deceased—hung from a post near a grave, and the breeze played music with the hollow pipes as I ducked out of the tunnel.

A familiar figure crawled in the dirt near an older tombstone unmarked by runes, magic, or metal, a trail of curly red hair flowing down her back.

"What the hell," I murmured, stepping forward. It was almost as if I'd conjured her with my thoughts. Except I hadn't expected to see her doing this.

Cressida Manos kneeled before the gravestone, her fingers covered in paint, her hands trailing streaks of neon colors over the stone. Small empty bottles lay strewn in the dirt around her. She giggled as she worked, completely unfazed by the mud coating her legs and bare feet.

"What the devil are you doing?" I demanded.

Cressida glanced up, but rather than be concerned or surprised by my presence, her giggles grew, her finger rising to her lips. "Shhh, I'm making them pretty."

My mouth fell open. "Who?"

"The dead." Plastering more paint on the stone, she hummed under her breath. "I thought they needed a little color."

"You thought?" Gripping her by the shoulders, I dragged her backwards. "Does this grave belong to your family?"

I knew it didn't. I knew all the graves in both sections of the cemetery by heart, but I was curious about her reply.

She twisted out of my grip and crawled away, mixing the paint on her hands with mud as she went. "It's nice to help out strangers. Don't you ever feel charitable?"

Something about the way she moved, her face full of unhinged glee, made me uneasy. She seemed like a completely different person. As if she were possessed. "This isn't charity. It's vandalism."

Laughing, she pushed herself to her feet, hugging herself, the gesture spreading paint and mud to her clothes. Streaks of it ran down the side of her face. She looked like a part of the earth, rising like fire and vengeance, and for the first time, I saw beauty.

I was insane.

"Vandalism?" She swayed on her feet. "Coming from the son of an outlaw, that's rich. Be a good boy and fetch . . . or, you know, something. Isn't that what dogs do? Can't you go to hell from here? I bet they have a nice big playground just for your kind."

I snorted in disbelief, my gaze locked on her face. Her green eyes were wild and unfocused. I didn't know much about Cressida Manos, but the things I'd heard and the few times I'd encountered her personally didn't match up with the girl I was facing now. This wasn't the girl who'd tried to protect me from getting in trouble. There was something evil about the girl I was facing now, and it triggered the hellhound inside of me.

"Yeah," I sneered, "there's a whole obstacle course for dogs down there. We heel, fetch, roll over, play dead, and occasionally, we breed."

My words caused her to freeze, her shocked gaze swinging to mine, her hand flying to her mouth. "Oh." A small giggle escaped, her palm turning the laugh into something like a sneeze. "Oh! You have a sense of humor. If a little misguided." She wagged a dirt-crusted finger at me. "You're funny."

I didn't laugh. "And you're drunk."

"No," she giggled louder, "not possible." She hiccupped. "I don't drink." Stumbling toward me, she rose up on her tiptoes, lifted her head, and breathed into my face. "See? Nothing."

She smelled like green apples and toothpaste.

"It's hard candy." She lost her balance, her hands shooting out, her fingers wrapping around my forearms. "It's good for focusing." Dropping one of her hands, she fished in the pocket of her cotton shorts before offering me a plastic-wrapped lump. "Watermelon or apple?"

Rather than accept the candy, I yanked my sunglasses off, stuck them on my T-shirt, and shook her loose before framing her face with my hands. Her head looked tiny sandwiched between my large palms, and I forced her to look at me.

My skin started to heat, and I struggled to keep it cool. No more burning. My control was better than that.

"What is this?" I asked.

Cressida stared at me, her eyes locked on mine, and it was like watching someone hit a light switch. The sarcastic, amused smile on her lips faded into a painful, confused frown. Her gaze widened, her lips moving silently. The same two words over and over until, finally, she managed a weak, "It hurts."

"What?"

"Your stare."

I released her so fast, we both stumbled backwards. "I thought oreads weren't affected by a hellhound's eyes." My mind raced. Burning her would be nothing compared to hurting her with my gaze. My dad wouldn't just be disappointed, he'd be furious. "Oreads can't be affected by a hellhound's eyes. You're immortal, right? Tell me my eyes can't hurt you. Tell me." Even I recognized the desperation in my voice. My dad wouldn't be the only one I'd have to deal with if I hurt someone in Havenwood Falls. I'd also have to deal with the Court.

"What are you talking about?" Cressida asked, bewildered. "Why are you here? What is this?"

I looked up to find her spinning in place, a completely freaked out expression on her face.

"What's going on?" She held her hands up, her eyes taking in the mud and paint. "What am I doing here?"

If I was confused before, it was nothing like the confusion that slammed me now. "What do you mean, what's going on? You were vandalizing a tombstone."

Cressida jerked her head toward me, her green eyes dull. "I wouldn't . . . I couldn't . . ."

I nodded at the grave.

She glanced at it, at the paint-smeared stone, and her hands started to tremble. "I wouldn't."

I took a step toward her. "You just did it. Are you telling me you don't remember?"

Her face filled with panic, and her breathing deepened, her thudding heartbeat calling out to the beast in me. It didn't help that I was still upset over the eyes thing.

"I'm telling you I didn't do it!" she cried, her voice shaking as badly as her hands. Her gaze dropped to her feet. "Where are my shoes? Why don't I have shoes on?"

Her fear and confusion engulfed me, twisting my pounding heart, and I reached out, smoothing her wild hair away from her face. "What kind of paint is that?"

She shied away from my touch. "What?"

"The paint," I repeated. "What kind is it?"

Taking a deep breath, she squinted at the empty bottles on the ground. "Acrylics."

I fought back a laugh. Even deranged and out of her mind, this girl didn't know how to properly break the law. "Well, that's fortunate. I don't think you've been here long enough for it to dry, and the stone was already damp. Help me clean it off."

Leaving her briefly, I went to my motorcycle and removed a bottled water and an extra white T-shirt I'd grabbed earlier in case I stayed overnight at the cemetery.

Returning, I threw her the water. "I'll scrub, you pour."

Catching the bottle easily despite her trembling hands, she twisted the lid off. Together, we kneeled before the headstone, my body completely dwarfing hers. I'd met her sister the day we made the delivery at Summit and Apex, and I didn't remember Leda Manos being this small. Or this ruffled.

Cressida dumped water onto the stone, and I scrubbed at it with the T-shirt, the paint coming off easier than I'd hoped. The nymph's heartbeat slowed as we worked, the work calming her, the thudding less prominent, less panicked.

"You think you can talk now?" I asked.

Leaning back, she glanced at me. "I don't know what happened. I didn't do this."

The girl who'd been painting the tombstone when I found her and the girl I was talking to now were two completely different people, despite sharing the same body.

Sighing, I met her gaze. My sunglasses still hung from my shirt, leaving my eyes naked, but she didn't shy away from my stare. The other girl—the strange, wild version of Cressida—had been hurt by it. "I believe you."

She froze, her throat working hard, swallow after swallow, and I knew she was trying not to cry. "Something is wrong with me."

That I couldn't help her with.

"At least you won't get in trouble for this," I said, perusing our handiwork.

Setting the water bottle down, she fisted her hands, her gaze roaming over the cemetery. Silence fell between us.

"Why are you here?" she asked finally.

Despite the mud, I sat back, feeling the damp ground seep in through the bottom of my jeans. I was already wet from the knees down. "I guess you could say I have a thing for hanging out with the dead."

"I've heard that about hellhounds." Cressida nodded, the movement so resolute it was like she was giving herself permission to do something. "Should we start over?" she asked.

Ah, so that's what she'd been talking herself into. "Start over?"

She offered me her dirt-covered hand. "Cressida."

I didn't take it. "I know your name. No need to reintroduce ourselves."

She glared. "It's a new start."

"Why?" I asked. "I don't think there's anything wrong with the old start."

For a long moment, she stared, and then—after coming to the same conclusion—her face changed, a smile stealing her unease. "I guess not." She gestured at the tombstone. "Thank you."

"Don't sweat it. Dawn'll be here soon. You need a lift home?"

"No, it's quicker for me by foot."

"Even without shoes?" Apparently I didn't know as much about oreads as she did about hellhounds.

"Even without those."

Standing, I brushed myself off. "All right, then. I guess that's my cue. Stay safe, nymph, and try to stay out of trouble. If you find out what happened tonight, please feel free to find me and let me know. The curiosity is killing me. You owe me that much. Deal?"

She gave me an absent look full of turmoil. "Deal."

Her unsettled expression made the beast in me bristle, and I groaned inwardly. I much preferred breaking the law to having the protector in me piqued. Once the protector inside of me was interested, I was screwed.

I had a bad feeling about tonight.

CHAPTER 7

CRESSIDA MANOS

*F*ollowing Jack Peters out of the cemetery, I watched as he straddled his motorcycle, giving me a final curious perusal before revving his engine and taking off into the night. He made an impressive figure in the dark, as impressive as he did in the daylight. It was comforting being near him. Somehow, I trusted him. After tonight, all the rumors about him seemed less like truth and more like conjecture. Then again, I'd overheard stories from his former one-nighters, and they'd been too detailed to be entirely false.

As soon as Jack was out of sight, I started shaking again, my body trembling uncontrollably. My hands fisted, my jaw clenching to keep my teeth from chattering, the tears I'd been holding back slipping down my cheeks. I stared at the cemetery's entrance, a whimper escaping my lips. What happened to me? Why had I come here?

Dread rising like a raging inferno inside of me, I left the grounds, making my way warily into the mountains and up the pass toward my house, faster than any human, but slower than normal for me. Even at night, eyes were everywhere in Havenwood Falls. Shifters prowled, vampires who found it hard to sleep paced into the late hours, and creatures who preferred the dark did gods knew what, as long as it didn't violate Court rules.

The sun was preparing for its trek across the sky when I made it home, and I rushed to rinse my feet with an outside water hose before sneaking inside. According to a clock hanging above our mantle, it was half past four in the morning, and I hurried upstairs, shedding my clothes in the bathroom before stepping into the shower. Water sluiced over my skin, steam rising, the liquid washing away the paint, mud, and shame. Time passed, my skin wrinkling in the water, my head hanging. Not all of the paint came off of my skin, and after finally stepping free of the shower, I dug a bottle of turpentine out of a small wooden desk in the corner of my room, a towel wrapped around me as I scrubbed at my hands.

"This is crazy," I whispered.

Slink jumped onto the desk, knocking the turpentine over, and I jerked off my towel to soak it up.

A light in the hallway switched on, and I dove for my dresser, pulling on an oversized old T-shirt and another pair of cotton shorts just as the door swung open.

"You okay in here?" Mom asked, entering. "I smell turpentine." I didn't have to look at a clock to know what time it was. Mom's schedule was a well-oiled machine, steady and unchanging, which meant she'd been busy in the kitchen while I spent an eternity shedding my shame in the shower.

I nodded, the towel on my head falling off in the process. I caught it. "Yep, all good."

She studied me, her brows arched, and even though there wasn't a hint of accusation in her gaze, my heart beat like a drum inside my chest, each thud full of guilt and terror.

It was suddenly too hot in the room, and I pulled at the collar of my shirt.

"What have I told you about—" Mom began.

I lost it. Completely lost it. "No, no, no! I take it back. I'm not good. Not good at all. Do you know what I did last night, Mom?" Wringing my hands, I paced the room. "I vandalized a tombstone with acrylic paints. Actual acrylics. Like that's a cool thing to vandalize anything with. In the middle of the night. In a cemetery." Pausing, I blew out a breath. "In the middle of the night. In a cemetery." Because I felt that was worth repeating.

Mom's eyes widened. "Cress—"

I slapped my forehead. "I don't even know how I got there. It was in that old part of the cemetery. The section for supernaturals." My words spilled out, along with all my burdens. I'd never been good at keeping things from my parents. "Ican'tevenrememberdoingitbut-Iwasthereand—"

Mom stepped toward me, her hand flying to her chest. "Mercy, Cressida, slow down. What is wrong with you? Did you have a bad dream?"

"No, Mom, I'm telling you I—"

"I never heard you leave the house, and you know how light a sleeper I am."

"Yeah, but, Mom, I—"

"Did you go to sleep as soon as you came up from supper? It's not good to doze off on a full stomach. Gives you bad dreams."

Frustrated, I moved past her to my small bathroom, swung the door open, and pointed at my discarded muddy clothes. "When did my nightmares suddenly involve mud wrestling?"

Mom gasped.

"There's something wrong with me," I told her. "I don't remember going to the cemetery, but I remember being there. I don't remember painting anything, but I remember seeing the tombstone with the paint on it."

I sounded like a crazy person.

Mom brushed past me and picked up the clothes. "Aren't you a little late for April Fools' Day? You're not making sense, sweetheart. Do you think you could have just gone outside? Everything is a little muddy after the rain."

My lips thinned. This was unbelievable. "Are you saying I sleepwalked? Can oreads even do that, Mom? Like, seriously? Can we? Because up until now, I rarely sleep, and I very rarely have any dreams at all."

Mom lifted my clothes, sniffed them, then lowered them again.

I scrunched my nose. "What are you doing? Trying to see if I rolled in something dead while at the cemetery?"

"Checking for alcohol or drugs. Even oreads can get drunk and high."

"Not funny, Mom."

She squinted at me. "Were you alone at the cemetery?"

I hiccupped, one violent hiccup after another, as if my body was vehemently trying to keep me from revealing the fact that I'd been with Jack Peters, bad boy extraordinaire. There was no way Mom would believe there'd been no drugs or alcohol involved if I mentioned him. Even though I was pretty sure he didn't do that kind of thing.

"Sure," I replied, hiccupping.

Mom circled me, sniffing. "This isn't like you. If anything, coming up with outlandish stories was more Leda's thing when she was your age."

My hiccups stopped. "This isn't a story!"

"Then why isn't anyone from the Court showing up at our door? You know if something was wrong with you, the tattoo and the wards in the town should have picked it up."

My whole body slumped. She had a point. "I don't know. Maybe I have some rare oread illness that hasn't been discovered yet. Something the tattoo or the Court's spells wouldn't know to pick up. Like when that virus got past our viral protection software last year, and we had to buy those new computers for the store." My eyes went wide. "I could be dying, and we wouldn't even know!" Rushing to the standing full-length mirror next to my closet, I pulled down my lower eyelids. "I should see a doctor, right?"

In the mirror, I watched Mom roll her eyes. *Seriously* roll her eyes. "Oreads can't get sick, Cressida." She peered at my reflection. "Have you taken a sudden interest in theatre? Is it like this weird obsession Leda suddenly has with the harp?"

I frowned. "I don't think you're hearing me, Mom."

Mom shook my clothes at me, mud and all. "Oh, I'm hearing you. Oreads have strong constitutions, and while we don't always have dreams or sleepwalk, it's not unheard of. But we *don't* get sick. If this is going to become a habit, we'll start bolting the door."

Ugh! I couldn't believe Mom wasn't getting it. Was her disbelief because I was *too* good a daughter? Is this what you got if you never broke the rules?

"Why?" I asked. "So I won't sleepwalk off a mountain? It's not like the fall would kill me."

"Smart-aleck behavior doesn't suit you, darling." Mom cradled my clothes and walked toward the door. "It's after six. Didn't you want to get some art in before the studio opens?"

I sighed, completely defeated. "Are you and Dad okay at least? Last night was weird."

Mom frowned. "We're fine. There's oatmeal on the stove. Brown sugar and butter, just like you like it."

She closed the door behind her, and I fell onto my bed, my gaze on the ceiling. Slink jumped onto my stomach and kneaded me with her paws. I was learning a very important lesson this morning. Sometimes being a supernatural in a supernaturally protected town could be a real pain. Especially if whatever was happening was completely impossible for an oread and somehow undetectable by the Court.

Pulling my pillow out from under my head, I stuffed it over my face and screamed. Had I been dreaming? I mean, could it be possible I had been sleepwalking, and then woken up when Jack found me?

The pillow fell to the bed. That made more sense than being sick.

I glanced down at Slink. "Why can't you be a talking cat? You know, like that one in the Japanese anime you watched with me the other day? A little ancient wisdom would be nice."

Lifting her paw, I pointed it at me, and made my voice echo, all childlike, off the walls. "Your mother is a six-hundred-year-old oread. You're getting nothing from the ancient wisdom department."

I hated it when my fake-talking cat was right.

CHAPTER 8

JACK PETERS

The first thing Pops always did when he wanted me to do something was pretend he gave a shit about the stack of books and DVDs I kept stuffed on a crooked shelf above my desk.

My bedroom at the MC clubhouse was a perfect square of chaos. Discarded clothes, loose change in a collection of empty grape soda bottles, a box full of pocket knives, stacks of magazines, and posters of half-dressed women were scattered everywhere: the floors, the walls, and under the bed. The posters hung like wallpaper, the pictures courtesy of the club. Not that I didn't appreciate them.

Pops stood at my desk when I walked in, a towel draped around my neck. I ran the rough fabric through my hair, soaking up the excess water in the strands while Pops ran his fingers down the titles on my shelf. All of them were history books and documentaries, texts and videos ranging from European to American history to stuff about forensic anthropology and archeology.

"Indiana Jones was a badass," Pops mumbled. This was his way of making himself feel better about my taste in literature. I should probably throw in a couple copies of porn.

"You didn't come in here to discuss the Pax Romana or the importance of overseas exploration," I said, yanking the towel off my neck and replacing it with a black band T-shirt. "What's up, Pops? If

47

you're interested in that sibling-comparison article, it's the fourth magazine down." I kicked at the stack next to my bed.

Liam massaged his forehead. "Sometimes I wonder if you came from my loins."

"Does the club know you talk like this?"

"This sparkling personality is reserved specifically for you."

"I'm honored. Really."

Pops grinned. "We're doing a run tonight out of town. Nothing too serious, so I'd like you to ride along. Observe."

I stared.

Pops cleared his throat. "You can't prospect until you finish school, but it wouldn't hurt for you to ride along on some of the less serious runs."

The finishing school thing was Pops's rule for his sons. It didn't apply to others. The general rule—outside of Taemin, me, and Cade—said anyone eighteen and older could prospect, high school diploma or no.

"Did you get this approved?" I asked.

"We voted on it in the last meeting. Minor stuff only."

I sat on the edge of my unmade bed, the black comforter trailing on the hardwood floor at my feet. "Pops—"

"Give it a shot, Jack. You don't have to make any decisions now, and you can always prospect after," he hooked his thumb at the shelf of books, "you're done playing Indiana Jones. You do realize I lived through part of this shit, right?"

Lowering my head, I snorted back a laugh, my hand rubbing the back of my neck. Pops was three hundred fifty years old, which was young for a hellhound. It wasn't like he was in a hurry to hand over the presidency. His outlaw days began in the golden age of piracy. He was forty-eight years old when he first met the famous Blackbeard. Pops especially liked telling that story when he was drunk. Repeatedly, as if it was supposed to get better with each telling. Truth was, I loved hearing it, but there was no way in hell I was telling him that. Liam Peters knew how to tell a story.

"Run tonight," Pops reminded me, moving to the door. "We ride at six o'clock sharp."

My thoughts drifted to Cressida and the weird night we'd spent in the cemetery. The shirt I'd used to clean the tombstone was safely tucked under my mattress, a freakish souvenir, the reminder causing a bud of unease to unfurl in my gut.

"I'm not sure tonight's good for me, Pops." Damn the protector in me. For some reason, I didn't want to be too far away from Cressida Manos.

"No school. No commitments. No excuses," Pops said firmly. "Six o'clock sharp." He left, leaving the door open behind him.

Standing, I pulled a cell phone I rarely used out of the drawer next to my bed, stuffed it into the pocket of my jeans, and followed Pops out the door.

The main room of the clubhouse closely resembled a tavern. A large area with scarred hardwood flooring, it was an open space with a long bar off to the side. A pool table rested in the center of the room surrounded by random tables and red-cushioned, metal-backed chairs. A jukebox sat against the side wall, a worn old couch sagging next to it. A big flat-screen television was anchored near the ceiling facing the room, and old neon beer signs hung along the walls. Two doors, one closed and the other propped open, led to a meeting room and a kitchen.

The smell of bacon wafted through the open door, and I grinned when a dark-haired woman in a tight dress and stiletto heels sauntered out of the kitchen, a plate of food resting in her hands.

Melaina Savage was everything a man could want in a woman and everything a man should be afraid of. The three-hundred-year-old sister of the MC club's vice president and a fellow hellhound, Melaina was the owner of Silk, a nightclub in town, and the only consistent female presence my brothers and I had following our mother's death.

Offering me the plate, she studied me, the red hue in her hazel eyes hidden by special contacts. "Don't think just because I'm feeding you right now that this shit's going to become habit."

I accepted the plate sheepishly. Melaina only showed up this early in the morning if Pops asked her to come. If it was possible for a hellhound to tuck his tail between his legs, I'd do it. "I'm man enough to admit I'm scared right now."

Her brows arched, amusement flirting with her red-stained lips. "What's this I hear about you burning the Manos girl?"

"Oh, shit," I groaned. Knowing Cressida was giving me all sorts of grief.

Melaina thumped me on the forehead with her manicured nails. "When did your daddy start letting you cuss like that?"

I laughed, backing away to shovel food in my mouth before I lost my chance to do it. "There ain't a single clean-mouthed Peters in this house."

"*Isn't*," Melaina corrected. "You're one of the smartest people I know. Don't let people think you're uneducated when you're not."

"Yes, ma'am."

"Now, about the Manos girl . . ."

I kept eating, taking my time swallowing before answering. "It was an accident."

Melaina's face hardened, her eyes blades of hazel steel. "We don't have accidents like that, Jack. We do well staying off the Court's bad side here in Havenwood Falls, and we want to keep it that way. We keep the bad business out of town and the good business in it, and we sure as hell don't abuse our powers."

"Maybe you should be talking to Cade."

"He's still learning," she pointed out. "While you're on the verge of becoming a member of the MC."

Appetite gone, I offered her the plate. "It really was an accident."

Her gaze softened. "You have a bright future ahead of you, Jack. Stay straight, okay? If you've got woman problems, just let me know. If there's one thing I know, it's women."

"Not this one," I mumbled under my breath. "I don't think anyone would understand this one." And that was an understatement. I knew a lot about women, too. Well, physically anyway.

Sudden interest flared in Melaina's gaze. "That sounded like a challenge."

"Nope," I said, shoving the plate at her. "Stay away from this one, please."

Her gaze dropped to the dish in my hand. "I know you haven't forgotten where the kitchen is."

I frowned. "Boy, you sure know how to melt a man's heart."

She laughed. "I don't melt men's hearts, sweetheart. I burn them. Figuratively speaking, so you don't get any ideas."

Her warning reminded me of Cressida, and I took a step toward Melaina, my gaze holding hers. I hadn't put my sunglasses on yet, and I was glad of it. "I promise not to make any more mistakes. Leave the Manos girl to me."

"I'm not that vicious, honey. Follow the rules, and I've got no interest in your love life."

A relieved sigh escaped me.

"I have to say, though, this is the first time I've seen you this torn up about a girl," she said thoughtfully. "I always figured you for the love-'em-and-leave-'em-type, like your daddy."

"This chick isn't one of my girls."

"Hmm," Melaina mused. "Guess that says it all right there." Heels clicking on the floor, she headed for the exit. "You know where to find me."

A chuckle escaped me, my gaze following her affectionately. "Hey, Melaina." She glanced back. "Thanks."

She winked, shoved the door open, and disappeared into the light beyond. We gave each other grief, but the club and the people connected to it were family. All of them.

CHAPTER 9

CRESSIDA MANOS

*C*offee Haven was bustling with early morning fatigued visitors when I took my place in line, my hands disappearing into the pockets of my shorts, the oversized shirt I wore so long in the front, it covered the shorts completely.

"You could try harder, you know?" Leda pointed out, taking her place in line behind me. "I swear it looks like you came to town in a sleep shirt and nothing else. It's embarrassing."

"It's comfortable." I rose up on my tiptoes, leaning in close to her ear so I could lower my voice. "And no bra."

Leda huffed in disgust. "There are people in here who can hear you, you know?"

I shrugged. "If they're that interested in what I'm wearing, they need to find a hobby."

Shoes thudded over hardwood floors, and I let my gaze wander over the room. Other than the art studio and animal shelter, Coffee Haven was my favorite place to be in Havenwood Falls. With historic built-in features, including a long marble counter, and strategically placed plants and crystals, Coffee Haven was a beacon of positive energy. Willow Fairchild, the shop's owner and a powerful empath fae, also displayed local art, everything from paintings to sculptures to photography. The large picture window in the front pulled in tons of natural light, creating a sense of warmth that chased away the recent shadows in my brain.

Sitting in their usual spot, the town gossips mingled over coffee, their heads bent close together. Irene Beckett, a retired schoolteacher and one scary old woman, eyed me curiously, the big glasses covering most of her face magnifying her gaze. Despite being a mortal woman, Irene knew entirely too much about the supernatural happenings in Havenwood Falls, but for some reason the Court let her knowledge slide. I wondered whether that was due to respect or fear.

"You're being judged," my sister hissed. "It's the attire." Leda tugged on the hem of her red blazer, the suit jacket a perfect match to her knee-length skirt. "We should go shopping together."

I threw her a look. "I'll stick to the oversized, marked-down stuff at Callie's Consignments. It's much more comfortable than the fancy stuff you get."

She blew out a breath, sending wisps of blond hair flying around her face, the strands falling artfully from her twisted updo. At least her hair listened to her. My hair was going through puberty, completely obstinate and hard to deal with.

"Hey, have you seen Dad this morning?" I asked her.

We moved forward in the line.

"Yeah, why?"

"There seemed to be some tension between him and mom last night. Like, not normal tension. They were arguing about jewelry. That jewel that was delivered the other day. The emerald. Dad even raised his voice about it."

Leda frowned, concern etching her brow. We might have been total opposites in appearance and personality, but we had one thing in common: family was everything. Oreads were a tight-knit species, friendly, accepting of each other—even though we liked to tease—and very close.

"That doesn't sound like them," Leda mumbled.

"Yeah, it wasn't like them at all. It was weird."

Leda squeezed my shoulder gently, the subject of my clothes completely forgotten. "I'll keep an eye on them."

A bright-eyed Willow Fairchild greeted us when we finally made it to the counter, her turquoise-blue gaze searching our faces, her silvery-blond hair highlighting blemish-free pale skin. A bright blue, sleeveless summer dress hugged her slender frame.

Pointing an elegant finger at me, she narrowed her striking eyes. "A tall caramel macchiato with an extra shot of syrup," her finger rose to my sister, "and a tall chai latte."

"Never fails," I said, grinning. Willow always made coming to the shop a personal experience. "How's the little one?" Willow had given birth to a daughter on the first day of school last year.

"Little," Willow replied, working on the order. "She's just starting to walk, and it's taking everything I've got not to wrap her in bubble wrap." She finished one of the orders and set it on the counter. "Caramel macchiato, extra syrup. How about the Manos family? I'm feeling some anxiety in the air this morning."

My stomach clenched. "Nothing we can't get past."

"Hmm." Willow set the second order on the counter. "Chai latte."

Leda pushed a twenty-dollar bill toward her. "I've got both of ours."

Accepting the money, Willow rang up the sale and offered Leda the change. "I would try meditation," she suggested. "Or something personally relaxing. Anxiety isn't good for your health."

"Thanks." Grabbing my coffee, I moved out of line, Leda on my heels. "What are you feeling anxious about?" I asked her once we were away from the crowded front.

Leda pulled the tab on her cup and blew on the steaming liquid. "Nothing."

"Liar." Pushing the shop's door open, I waited for Leda to brush past me. "Mom said something about a new girlfriend."

"What?" Leda spun, mouth opening and closing, a cough bursting out of her lips. "I think I swallowed a fly." Her words came too quick, muffled, and overly eager. She rubbed her throat. I wasn't the only Manos bad at lying.

My lips twitched. "You know flies are born in poo and garbage, right?"

Leda coughed harder. "Seriously, Cressida."

"Just trying to make you feel better."

"I'm reveling in your sisterly warmth and affection." Lifting her cup, she saluted me. "I'm off. No rest for the weary."

"Said no oread ever," I chirped, watching her walk away. She was definitely thinking about someone, and even though I knew she was worried about what I'd said about our parents, I didn't think it was Mom and Dad she was thinking about. Pedestrians eased around me, and I leaned against a lamppost near the coffee shop to get out of their way.

In the distance, the rumble of a motorcycle rose on the wind, and I stiffened, my hands clutching the warm biodegradable cup. The rumble grew louder, and I knew even before the bike came around the bend that the rider was Jack Peters. Maybe it was instinct, or maybe I knew he wouldn't be able to let our night at the cemetery go that easily.

Pulling his motorcycle to a stop at the curb, Jack straightened, his sunglasses-covered eyes searching the area. His leather cut rested over a black T-shirt that hugged his biceps and revealed more of the tattoos on his arms.

I nearly strangled my cup, my eyes glued to him as he lifted his head and inconspicuously sniffed the air. His chin lowered, his face turning my way, and I fought the urge to hide. There was something predatory about Jack Peters.

After removing his helmet and kicking down his stand, Jack climbed off the motorcycle, checking the street before jogging across. Pedestrians stared at him, some of them students from my school, and I sunk as far into the lamppost as I could get.

"You aren't easy to find," Jack said when he was within earshot.

"I didn't know you were looking."

He came to a stop next to me. "I figured we should talk."

Through the window of Coffee Haven, I saw Irene Beckett press her face against the glass, her mouth moving so fast, the gossips next to her—Biddie Half-Moon and Laverne and Sybil Carson—didn't stand a chance of keeping up. This was going to be all over town by nightfall.

"Not here," I murmured, wincing at the grin and little wave Irene Beckett threw my way. "Let's meet at the studio."

"I'll walk with you," Jack offered.

I froze. "You don't need to move your bike?"

"It's just down the street, Manos." He grinned, the smile wicked. "Why? Are you afraid of being seen with me?"

Pushing away from the lamppost, I marched down the sidewalk. "Depends on who you ask. Your reputation precedes you."

"Ah," he fell into step beside me, "so you're worried people will think you're sleeping with me."

It was a statement rather than a question, the ease with which he said it speaking volumes, and embarrassed heat flooded my face. "I didn't mean—"

"Don't even try to remove your foot from your mouth," he said, amusement coloring his words. "It would only be a problem if I was ashamed of it. There's nothing wrong with what I do. Considering I'm walking with a potential criminal at the moment, I'd say we're even. Except," he nudged me, "people don't exactly know you have a wicked side, do they?"

"I don't have a wicked side."

We approached Apex Art Studio, and I ducked past the window of Summit Jewelry to keep from being seen from inside. Jack kept walking, completely nonplussed.

"I think you're ashamed of me," he teased.

Sliding my studio key into the lock, I entered the space, letting him brush past me before shutting and bolting the door. "Why would I be ashamed? Technically, we don't even know each other."

"Says the girl who needed me to get her out of trouble last night."

"Can you just stop? That wasn't me. I don't know what that was." I switched on the overhead lights and inhaled the scent of paint and disinfectants. "I told my mother."

Jack pulled off his sunglasses, his red-hued gaze locking with mine. Alone, he seemed so much larger than he'd seemed out on the street. Dangerous, even. "Wow, you commit a crime, and then you admit it to your parents." He shook his head. "Who are you?" Sarcasm dripped off his words.

I was too caught up in my own thoughts to care. "She didn't believe me."

That got his attention. "What?"

"Apparently, if you're a good enough daughter, it's hard to convince people to believe you're bad." Crossing my arms, I closed my eyes and inhaled deeply. "There's also the fact that oreads don't get sick and that neither my tattoo nor the wards alerted the Court. Final deduction: I was sleepwalking."

Silence fell, and I opened my eyes to find Jack studying my face. "She really didn't believe you?"

"Even after I showed her the muddy clothes."

"Wow, I think I'm doing something wrong with my life. I sneeze too loud, and I've suddenly got a dozen fingers pointing at me."

"Must suck for you."

"I hear the condescension in your voice, and I choose to ignore it." He glanced around the studio, his gaze passing over the yellow walls, unpainted pottery, and empty canvases. "I thought this place didn't open until one?"

"I work on personal art when it's closed."

Sipping on the coffee in my hands, I peered at Jack over the rim of my cup. Without his sunglasses on, he looked less menacing somehow. More boy than beast. Or maybe he was just growing on me.

"Do you think you were sleepwalking?" His question came out of nowhere.

I let my gaze drop to the floor. "It's not unheard of with oreads. Mom says, anyway. So it seems the most logical explanation."

Jack swore under his breath, the words "not fucking likely" audible through his growl. "Look, I'm going to be out of town tonight. Do you have a cell phone?"

My gaze shot up. "Yeah, why?"

"Give me the number." Pulling a phone out of his pocket, he handed it to me. "Service sucks in this town, but texts seem to work better."

"No, they don't."

"Just put your number in, Manos."

I pulled up his contact list and added my name. "Why are you doing this?"

He took the phone from me, and then pressed the number I'd just added. From a desk in the corner of the room, my phone began to ring. I usually left it at the studio hooked up to the charger and didn't bother with carrying it home.

"Now you have my number."

"Why are you doing this?" I repeated.

Jack tucked his phone back into his jeans. "You don't really know any hellhounds, do you? Not too personally anyway, right?" When I didn't respond, he leaned forward. "You were in trouble last night, and it triggered something. The hellhound in me wants to protect you. Once that protective gene gets sparked, it's a bitch to try to ignore." He grimaced. "Lucky me."

"Oh, gods!" I gaped at him. "We're not like bonded now or something, are we? Because from what Dad's told me about your kind, I didn't think you did that. I'm not sure how much you know about oreads, but we're really not all that into—"

Reaching out, he placed his fingers against my lips. "We're not anything. Feeling the need to protect someone has nothing to do with . . . that. Hellhounds are essentially bodyguards when the need arises. If we bonded with everyone we protected, things would get a little awkward."

He dropped his hand, and I sucked in my cheeks. This whole thing was still awkward. Very, very awkward.

"Is that what you do?" I asked. "I mean, when you're not in school? You're a bodyguard?"

He laughed, the sound harsh. "Not exactly. That's more my Pops's thing right now. I do odd jobs for my father's delivery company, and I bide my time."

"Until what?"

"Graduation."

"Oh." Speechless, I moved away from him, keeping myself busy by collecting the supplies I needed to work on a new piece of pottery.

Jack watched, his gaze tracking my movements.

I pulled the studio apron on over my clothes. "Do you want to try?"

He backed toward the door. "Nah, I should go. Look, just keep your cell with you tonight, okay?"

I watched him leave, an odd hollow sensation forming in my chest. It almost felt like . . . I missed him. Which was weird and completely . . . I mean, was it weird?

My cell phone dinged.

Racing to grab it off the desk, I opened my messages.

Keep the phone with you, Manos.

Adding his number to my contact list, I hugged the phone, a smile playing on my lips.

"What's wrong with you?" I asked, slapping myself gently in the face. "It's just a message. A stupid, overbearing, completely dictatorial message." Staring at it again, I fought a smile. "Just a message. Get a grip."

My mouth, brain, and heart weren't even remotely communicating with each other.

A guy had asked for my number. I grinned like a fool.

CHAPTER 10

JACK PETERS

*E*vening came too quickly, the anxiety I felt over the Cressida situation stealing the hours in the day. I'd barely gotten a chance to check in with her when six o'clock rolled around. Pops gathered four of his men, sending his VP, along with his most trusted club members, on a more difficult run while the rest of us straddled our motorcycles, helmets on and engines rumbling.

We hit the road at six sharp. A delivery truck preceded us, and I fell to the back of the group as we rode out, my tires eating the asphalt beneath me. The mountains loomed before us, starkly beautiful in the late afternoon. Like sleeping giants curled into a fetal position.

Silence and wind. That was the tale of the road. Stark, lonely, and beautiful. The sun began to set as we cruised forward, streaks of orange, pink, and purple blooming across the sky like fireworks. Riding with a club was all about rank—the higher your seniority, the further up the line you rode. Being a potential prospect, I was nothing more than a hang-around, but I didn't mind pulling up the rear.

I enjoyed the trip, letting the wind massage my scalp, its chilly fingers pulling the cobwebs out of my brain. As a minor, I should have been wearing a helmet, but breaking the law wasn't something my father sweated, especially when I appeared old enough to be without one. An accident wouldn't kill me either, and I enjoyed the wind, so I didn't always follow the rules.

My father once told me being on the road was a lot like being married. Exhilarating, unexpected, and full of unseen obstacles. Navigating it was like making love to a woman. How far you made it depended on how much of yourself you were willing to give up. Pops was a philosopher at heart.

The roads were steep and winding, the darkening horizon a bruising wall of trees and cliffs, meadows and valleys. For me, it was all about the ride. I didn't need a destination. There was something beautiful about not knowing where I wanted to go.

A little over two hours later, with miles and miles of road and Havenwood Falls behind us, we entered Montrose, the roads growing bumpier as we pulled through intersections, under lights, and past a group of warehouses, each more run down than the next.

It was after eight o'clock when we finally pulled into a parking lot. A group of men, all of them in leather cuts, waited on us. They straightened when we approached, a couple of them throwing cigarettes to the ground before grinding the butts into the asphalt.

Pops waved me to the side, and I parked away from the group, leaning back on my bike to wait. I was a bystander, a long-distance observer, only along for the ride. Participating in business was an earned privilege.

Pops dismounted, removed his bike gloves, and shook hands with a burly, bearded man. The guy smelled like a human, fear and adrenaline rolling off him in waves, the scent of drugs permeating his clothes. It was a wretched smell, and one of the reasons most hellhounds didn't indulge in much outside alcohol and weed.

I laughed under my breath. If only Cressida could see me now. Our lives couldn't be any more different. The people we called friends and the family we shared our homes with were nothing alike.

Why do you care? The question echoed in my brain, and I massaged my temples.

After a brief meeting in the parking lot, Pops disappeared into a warehouse, his head bent near the bearded guy's, the two of them in deep discussion. I could hear every word they said, but I tuned out the conversation, because the less I knew about my father's business dealings, the better off I was. Especially if I chose not to prospect with the MC.

Time passed, and I climbed off my bike, making my way into a barren field next to the parking lot, the beast in me restless.

Pulling my cell phone out of my pocket, I texted Cressida.

Jack: Everything okay?

Her response was quick.

Cressida: All good.

I dropped the phone back into my pocket, hooked my thumbs in my belt loops, and looked up at the sky. A blanket of stars stared down at me. When I was a little boy, before my mother died, she'd told me the stars were a minefield of explosives. That if a person could touch them, they'd immediately detonate and dissolve. Stars, she said, weren't meant to be handled. They were only meant to be enjoyed. Now that she was gone, they didn't look the same. Sometimes I wished I could touch them, to see how many of them I could destroy. Not because I wanted to get rid of the stars, but because I wanted to prove my mother was right.

Laughter rolled into the night from the parking lot, and I shook myself, digging once more for my phone to check the time. I really needed to start wearing a watch. An hour had passed.

The beast in me howled, feeling caged and helpless. This part of being a hellhound bugged me. Not that I didn't want to care for people, but once I got worried, it literally consumed me, turning me into an obsessive creature hell-bent on keeping someone safe.

I texted Cressida again.

Jack: What are you up to?

Five minutes passed with no response, and I began to pace the field, kicking at the dirt and rocks beneath my combat boots.

Jack: Did my message go through?

Another ten minutes. Still no response. The hairs on the back of my neck stood on end, the hellhound within howling. He didn't like not knowing how she was. *I* didn't like not knowing how she was. Although I referred to the hellhound within me as "he," the beast and I were one and the same.

"Let's ride," Pops called.

My bike had never felt so good. I'd also never been so tempted to eschew tradition and ride ahead of the group. We may be outlaws, but Pops had drilled responsibility into every single one of us so deeply, we'd become one with the word. A well-oiled machine.

The itch to get home must have been strong for all of us because we rode faster going back in than we had coming out. I wondered if the way I felt now was the same urgency people felt when hellhounds were after them, when the hounds of hell were on their trail. Literally.

Slowing at a traffic light, we pulled to a stop, and I dug my phone out.

The screen blinked, a message waiting, and I scrambled to open it.

Cressida: I'm in trouble.

My heart skipped a beat.

Jack: Where are you?

She didn't reply.

The light turned green, and we took off. My pulse raced, and I counted my breaths to keep my skin cool and my temper under control.

Guilt ate at me, and I didn't know if it was because my beast wanted to protect Cressida, or if it was because I was starting to really care about her.

Her too-slim body, unruly red hair, and small face filled my thoughts, and I scoffed. There was no way I was interested in her. Was I? The way she smiled, and the way she'd tried protecting me when I burned her also raced through my brain, and I sucked in a breath. Was I?

Worry ate away at my gut, her message ringing in my head. *I'm in trouble.*

CHAPTER 11

CRESSIDA MANOS

*T*all, lean, and intimidating, Deputy Tate Kasun studied me, his dark eyes sparkling with humor despite the police station's low lighting and the absolutely insane position we were both in.

"I feel like this is one of those television shows where, at any moment, someone is going to jump out and say this is all a prank." He tapped a pen in front of me. "Cressida Manos, of all people."

"I'm guessing it wouldn't help to say it wasn't me?" I posed it as a question.

Tate leaned back in his chair, pulling at the collar of his uniform, his foot tapping the station's hardwood floors. "I think what we have to remember here is how absolutely brilliant your life of crime is. Not only did you get the spray paint from your own family's store, you paid for it. *Paid* for it. I can't decide if you are the most honest criminal I've ever brought in, or the least logical."

I pouted. "This doesn't feel very professional, Deputy Kasun."

"My sister would agree, but then she'd probably have a lot to say about you sitting in this chair right now."

A member of my graduating class at Havenwood Falls High, Willa Kasun was Tate Kasun's younger sister and a shapeshifting wolf. All of the Kasuns were. My life was becoming canine-complicated, from getting caught by a hellhound in a cemetery to being arrested by a wolf while graffitiing two businesses in Miller's Plaza. The worst part? I couldn't remember committing the crimes. Unless you count the part where I came to covered in incriminating evidence and holding empty spray cans while outside a business in a halo of flashing police lights.

Weren't there reality shows less dramatic than this?

The door to the police station flew open, and my parents walked in, both frowning. Tate and I stood simultaneously.

My dad's eyes fell to my hands. "Really, Tate, handcuffs?"

Tate shrugged. "If you're going to have an interesting story to tell at school, you might as well go big."

Did I mention how much I loved Tate Kasun? Except maybe the whole "he arrested me" thing. He was much nicer than his jerk of a brother, Conall.

My gaze flew to my mother. "I told you I did it!"

Interest piqued, Tate glanced between us. "Is that a confession?"

"No!" I sputtered, my eyes flying anywhere and everywhere to avoid his gaze. The room blurred, the tan-colored walls and wooden blinds giving the place a warmer feel than any police station had the right to have. "I just meant that . . . that . . . ugh!"

Mom approached me, her auburn hair pulled away from her face. A loose button-up tunic, the buttons haphazardly done up, rested over a pair of khaki slacks.

"I'm telling you something is wrong with me," I told Mom before she could reach me.

She closed her eyes, inhaled, and then opened them again. "Talk to us, Deputy."

Tate remained standing. "I got a call from some locals who said they saw someone vandalizing property, and I found your daughter spray painting the outside of VIP Nails and Long & Associates CPA. Not only are there witnesses, but I caught her in the act, and so did my dash cam. You can't get better evidence than that." He glanced at me. "Fortunately for your daughter—"

"Cressida," I inserted.

"Not now," Dad warned me.

I pinched my lips together. Father's Day was right around the corner, and I wasn't exactly making this year a brilliant one.

"Fortunately for your daughter," Tate continued, "both Dao Pham and Brian Long are willing to not press charges, as long as she promises to clean up the graffiti." He sighed. "I've already notified the Court."

We all knew what that meant. Because I was a supernatural, any crime I committed would be reviewed by the Court of the Sun and the Moon. Consisting of the leaders of the Old Families, the Court's main purpose was to maintain peace in the town, especially among the supes, while ensuring the town's supernatural secrets were protected. This was the reason the supernatural residents were required to sign into the Court Registry and receive a tattoo.

"Because she's a minor and because Pham and Long are willing to waive the charges, I doubt she's going to have to stand before a formal review, but I'd expect to at least hear from Addie or Saundra Beaumont."

My father nodded. "Does this mean she can leave with us now?"

Tate made a show of undoing my handcuffs. "I have no reason to hold her." Nodding at me, he added, "Make sure you show up tomorrow morning to clean up those storefronts. I don't care how long it takes you. You got lucky this time."

Rubbing my wrists, I looked at him. "What if I *want* to talk to the Court? What if I think something is wrong with me?"

Tate's eyes narrowed, lips pursing thoughtfully. "I can put in a request, but I don't doubt they'll be contacting you themselves."

"Wait a minute," Mom protested. "I told you, Cressida, if it was anything worse than sleepwalking, we'd know by now."

It wasn't that Mom wanted to avoid the Court, but everyone in Havenwood Falls had a healthy dose of fearful respect for the Court members. Unless conditions warranted, it was better to remain under the radar.

"Sleepwalking?" Tate asked, surprised.

"Oreads can have vivid dreams," Mom told him.

Tate laughed. "Who knew your mind was so full of mischief, Cressida?"

Dad threw him a look.

Tate cleared his throat, his fingers pulling at his shirt. It looked like it was suffocating him. "Well, then, that does it. I'll finish filling out the report, and if you want to avoid charges, make sure you show up at Miller's Plaza on time."

"She'll be there," Mom promised, resting her hand on my back, not so gently urging me toward the door. We'd barely cleared the entrance when she turned on me. "Cressida Gwen Manos, I swear to th—"

"I feel like swearing might not be the best idea at the moment," I interrupted. Mom glared, and I took a step back. "But then again, if it makes you feel better."

Dad pinched the bridge of his nose. "What were you thinking?"

"I wasn't," I protested. "I'm telling you, it wasn't me!"

"Then how do you explain what just happened? They told us they had you on video."

We were so caught up in our heated debate that none of us saw or heard the motorcycle pull up to the police station.

"Hey," Jack's deep, familiar voice inserted. "Everything okay?"

My parents' horrified gazes slid slowly—ever so slowly—to the leather-vested biker on the sidewalk. Relief and dread filled me. Relief because I was glad to see him. Dread because I wasn't quite sure how to explain him to my parents.

Dad spoke first. "What's this?"

Jack pulled off his sunglasses, his gaze finding my face.

"Is this the trouble you meant?" he asked, nodding at the police station.

I tilted my head. "It happened again."

Mom's eyes widened, her gaze flicking between us, her body frozen.

"I . . ." She paused, shook her head, and covered her eyes with her palms. "I'm going to remove this hand, and when I open my eyes, we're going to be back at home and this is all going to be a bad dream."

Silence.

She dropped her hand.

I forced a smile. "Surprise?"

Mom took a fortifying breath. "You're still here. He's still here. *We're* still here."

My father's absolute refusal to move or speak completely freaked me out.

"Breathe, Dad," I prompted.

His face turned red, the flush so unexpected, I stumbled away from him, the move taking me closer to Jack.

In a deliberately low, menacing tone of voice, Dad gritted out, "What. Is. This?"

I bit my lip. "You know how I told you I painted that tombstone in the cemetery?"

"No," Dad answered.

"Yes," Mom replied.

They looked at each other.

"What? Why didn't you tell me this?" Dad asked.

Mom's hands found her hips. If she'd touched any other spot on her body, I wouldn't have worried, but her hips were a bad, bad sign.

I waved my hands at my parents, garnering their attention before their trivial debate turned into a full-blown argument. If I thought introducing them to Jack was scary, seeing them fight was even more terrifying. "This is Jack Peters."

My parents didn't return the introduction.

Dad offered a tight smile. "I've heard of him."

Sure he had.

I suddenly wanted to do the whole "cover my eyes and take a time out" thing my mom was so fond of.

"Jack's the one that found me painting the tombstone in the cemetery," I revealed. "Before he helped me clean it up." Mom's lips parted, and I rushed to add, "In my defense, I *did* tell you what happened."

Mom snorted. "Not everything."

"Minor detail."

Stepping toward Jack—who was now standing next to his bike—Mom perused him, her gaze rising up, up, up until it finally landed on his red-hued eyes. "Doesn't look minor."

A muscle in Jack's jaw jumped, and I could tell he was trying very, very hard not to laugh.

"And here I was worried about you," he hissed.

My head shot up. "You were?"

"Okay," my dad scrubbed his face, "why don't we go home, sit down, and talk some things over? I think I need a full detailed description and a drink before," he glanced at Jack and winced, "I can process this properly." Gesturing at Mom and me, he added, "You and you, come with me. You," he pointed at Jack, "stay here."

"Yes, sir." A smile escaping, Jack's gaze dropped to my hip and the outline of my phone. I patted the pocket of my shorts. Even though Tate had arrested me, he'd let me keep my phone. I'm sure part of that had to do with the handcuffs and the victims not pressing charges.

It was going to be a long night.

Trailing after Mom and Dad, I slipped my phone out, quickly typing two words before pressing send.

No matter how much I tried to hide my unease with humor, I couldn't shake the fear that gripped me.

There was no way I was sleepwalking.

CHAPTER 12

JACK PETERS

*C*ressida: **I'm scared.**

Those two words did me in, my gaze locked on the phone in my hand, on the scratched-up screen, and the words I couldn't let go of. Despite being nothing more than letters on a backlit surface, Cressida's text was packed with emotion.

The drive back to Havenwood Falls after the out-of-town run had been trying enough knowing Cressida was in trouble, but to find out she'd committed another crime—albeit minor compared to the stuff I'd done and to the shit I knew my father was involved in—made my head hurt with niggling questions and doubts. Sleepwalking, my ass. Still, it was a relief knowing she was okay, that she'd been dragged in by Tate Kasun, the more easygoing of the Kasun crew, and that her parents had cared enough to rush over.

A voice in my head, one all hellhounds were familiar with, tossed warnings out at me like bread crumbs. Looking at it from a logical standpoint, Cressida's mom was right. It really did look like she was sleepwalking, going into town and committing crimes she'd never attempt if she was awake, as if sleep removed all of her inhibitions and set her free from the expectations and rules that normally regulated her life.

Only one problem with that scenario: Cressida *liked* the rules. It didn't take knowing her well to gather that. She enjoyed being Cressida, following a set schedule and carrying her portion of the weight in life and work. I didn't think sleep would change that.

Slipping onto my bike, I rode through the maze of roads, down one street and up another, until I glided into the MC parking lot. Lights shone brightly from inside, the glare spilling out into the night. Music spilled out with it, the occasional shout and "hell, yeah" carried away on the breeze as men and women weaved in and out through the door. The smells of alcohol and sex were ripe on the air.

I lounged in the shadows, watching and waiting. I wasn't in the mood for a party.

My younger brother stumbled into the night, high on life and too much sugary soda—Pops was lenient, but not when it came to alcohol —and I snorted back a laugh as he cocked his hip against the corner of the building and reached for his pants.

"You piss on the side of that building and Pops is going to tear you a new one," I called out.

Cade squeaked, fell against the brick, and then pushed himself away, running his hands down his clothes as if nothing out of the ordinary had happened.

"Holy shit, Jack!" he fumed. "I'm not the only one who pisses out here."

"You want to make a bet on that, or would you rather find out what scrubbing brick during the summer at dawn is like? Trust me on this one. Been there, done that."

Cade sniffed. "What are you doing out here anyway?"

"Not much for celebrating tonight."

"Whatever." Cade's expression went from nonchalant to pissed off. It was like that a lot lately. Fourteen was a hell of an age for hellhounds. "I don't get it. You get to do shit with the club Pops wouldn't even dream of letting me do, and instead of reaping the rewards, you sulk in the dark."

"Don't start," I warned.

Cade ignored me. "They even have your favorite grape soda. And because it's you, I bet they let you have the alcohol."

"And that's why Pops hasn't let you do much for the club yet. By the time you get your bike, you need to learn control and realize how little half of this shit," I gestured at the party, "matters. What matters is the brotherhood, not what you can reap from it."

Cade looked away, his sunglasses picking up the glare from the security lights near the company warehouse. No matter how much we tried to get along lately, my brother and I spent more time arguing than seeing eye to eye.

Changing tactics, I rubbed a hand along my jaw. "Talk to me about Cressida Manos."

Cade's head jerked my way. "Dude! Why?"

By the way he bristled, I could already tell this conversation wasn't going to go well, but I forged on. "Some weird shit is going down with her lately, and I'm trying—"

"You don't get to hit that," Cade interrupted. "She's nowhere close to the kind of girls you hang out with anyway."

I scowled. Was my reputation really that bad? First, Cressida was worried about walking down the street with me, and now my own brother was warning me away from a girl my own age. "I'm not hitting anything, and if I was, I don't need your permission. Right now all I care about is protecting her."

The anger on Cade's face momentarily wavered. "From what?"

"That's what I'm trying to figure out. She was arrested tonight."

Cade gawked. "Cressida Manos? Arrested? No way!"

"Yeah, I didn't get there in enough time to find out why, but I have an idea."

Pulling his sunglasses down, Cade peered at me over the rim. "Are you talking with her? Like, as in fully checking her out? As in interested in her for more than a tumble in the sheets?" Sometimes he didn't talk like a fourteen-year-old.

This was it. "And if I am?"

Cade kicked at the gravel at his feet. "Damn it, this isn't fair, bro."

I laughed, the sound harsh. It took everything I had not to tell him how ridiculous I thought his crush was. Then again, maybe that's why it annoyed me so much. At only fourteen, he'd noticed Cressida's charms, while everyone else overlooked them simply because of her outward appearance and her too-bubbly personality.

"Look, I stumbled on her at the cemetery the other night, and something about how desperate she seemed really got to my beast, okay? You know as well as I do, once the beast is interested, there's no backing down. So, can you do me a favor? If you notice anything unusual, let me know."

"Is it just the beast?" Cade asked quietly. "Is this really just a protection run?"

And here was the real reason for approaching my brother. Hellhounds didn't like dealing underhanded with their own families. No matter what kind of shit we got involved in with the club or outside of it, we stayed honest with each other.

"It's not just the beast," I admitted. Something about Cressida had sparked my interest, and out of respect for my brother and his wide-eyed crush, I wanted to lay it all on the line.

Cade shrugged. "It's none of my business."

Grunting, I turned to walk away.

"Wait," Cade called. I paused, my back to him. "Thanks for being honest."

I'd just seriously complicated our relationship, but at least I hadn't lied. At least I wasn't hiding anything.

CHAPTER 13

CRESSIDA MANOS

*T*here wasn't anything more terrifying than my parents when they combined forces, allied together against one common enemy.

The way they stared at me now turned my blood to ice. I didn't often think about how old my parents were. I mean, it's not like I set an alarm every morning to remind myself that they'd lived for over six centuries.

Tonight, I saw the age in their eyes, and the history that we rarely discussed—like the fact that they'd lived in Paris during the whole bloody guillotine era—was right there in their gaze, all sharp steel and fire.

"So, before we get started, are we mad that I got arrested or that I am acquainted with Jack Peters?" I asked, standing uncertainly in the living room. They sat on our coffee-colored couch, elbows on their knees, fingers steepled.

I was dead.

"Let's start with Jack," Mom began.

"Let's not," Dad mumbled.

My parents had never looked at me the way they looked at me now. Sudden panic squeezed an overly excessive confession out of my mouth, each word tumbling out one after the other, all in one breath.

"I am not doing drugs." For some reason, I felt like that was an important distinction to make right off the bat. "'Cause, you know, I don't want you to get the wrong idea or anything. I also don't drink. So, the whole me painting stuff at night thing has nothing to do with alcohol. And if you think Jack Peters has anything to do with it just because he showed up all friendly-like tonight, he doesn't. I swear. Really. I've maybe known him a few days."

I held up two fingers, three, and then dropped them all together. "Well, I mean, I've known *about* him for forever, but we haven't been friendly. *If* we're even friends." My brows furrowed. "Actually, I'm not sure what we are, except that he helped me clean paint off a tombstone. Oh!" I held up my hand. "He *did* ask for my number. Which is kind of like a move, right? I mean, guys don't ask for your number if they don't want to talk to you. Or at least, I wouldn't think so. So, maybe he's interested. Which would be kind of nice . . . I mean . . . nah, maybe not."

Mom and Dad stared at me, horrified.

My pulse quickened, and logically, I knew I needed to shut up, but the words kept spilling forward. A flood of complete humiliation. "I'm not having sex, if that's what you're worried about. I mean, I haven't even—"

"That's enough!" Dad roared, storming to his feet.

I froze, my mouth opening and closing like a fish desperate for water, before tentatively asking, "Too much?"

Mom massaged her forehead. "A little too much."

Dad began pacing the living room. "For a moment, let's forget about Jack Peters, drugs, alcohol, and whatever else. What about this graffiti stuff?"

Mom stood and began pacing with him. In unison. It was creepy. "She has to be sleepwalking. I'm not sensing any magic."

A knock sounded on the door, and we all paused, as if caught in the headlights of a car. It was the middle of the night. No one had visitors in the dead of night. Except maybe vampires . . . or nocturnal supernaturals.

"You get it," Mom whispered.

Dad didn't move.

Our front door opened.

"It's me," my sister called, the door slamming behind her. She rounded the corner, a young woman with light brown hair, black-framed glasses, and a diamond nose ring following on her heels. "Oh, and Addie Beaumont," Leda added off-handedly, amusement clear in her voice.

Mom gasped.

Adelaide "Addie" Beaumont was the granddaughter of Saundra Beaumont, a powerful witch of one of the founding families of the Luna Coven. Saundra also served on the Court of the Sun and the Moon, which meant her granddaughter, Addie, was here on business.

Dressed in a pair of ripped jeans and an old T-shirt with the logo "I'm not a witch, you're a witch" plastered across it, Addie offered us a smile. "I guess you know why I'm here?"

"So soon?" Mom asked faintly. "Now?"

Leda, who managed to look elegant even when dressed down in a tank top and skinny jeans, leaned against our sofa, arms crossed. "I'm just here for moral support. I ran into the witch on the way here."

We all ignored her.

"I hear there was a special request," Addie said, her gaze swinging to me.

I chose this moment to completely embarrass myself as an oread.

Without any thought as to how I would look, I sat down hard on the floor, lifted my leg, and pointed at my tattoo. "Check it, if you don't mind. I really do think something is wrong with me."

"Cressida!" Mom gasped.

She said it like I was doing something scandalous. It wasn't like I didn't know Addie. Anyone in Havenwood Falls with a Court-issued tattoo had to meet Addie Beaumont at some point. She was the tattoo artist who did the magic-infused designs.

Horror widened my eyes. "I mean, not that I think you messed up or anything."

Addie laughed. "I gotta say, it's refreshing when the perpetrator is this willing to work with me." She crouched before me, her gaze dropping to the elegant chain charm bracelet tattooed around my ankle. "But there's nothing wrong with your tattoo, Cressida. The tat is only part of what protects the supes in this town. We have wards and protection spells for that, too. Nothing has been set off. I checked around before coming here. Even with the empaths. Willow Fairchild said she saw you and your sister at Coffee Haven, but all she felt was anxiety."

Guilt washed over me. "You checked with them tonight? As in, in the middle of the night?"

Addie winked. "They're used to it. Problems tend to arise more at night than during the day. It's part of the job." She glanced at my parents. "We're looking into some things, but right now we're stumped. According to Tate's report, she spray-painted two buildings but claims she can't remember doing it, despite being seen by witnesses, by him, and by his dash cam."

In two days, I'd learned a lot about a life of crime. Most importantly, I'd learned there was a very exact two-step process. First, people talked *to* you. Then, they talked *about* you.

Addie stood. "According to the evidence, she's guilty, but since the victims aren't pressing charges, we're going to skip a formal review and look into this more quietly. The Court is swamped." She chuckled. "And here we thought summer would be slow and quiet." Her gaze swung back to me. "Tate mentioned sleepwalking. Is this common for oreads?"

Mom wrung her hands. "Not common, but not unheard of. There was a case I saw personally about two hundred years ago." She winced. "In Italy. In that instance, the young man stripped naked and sang in the town square, but then couldn't remember it the next day."

"What happened to him?" I asked.

Mom's grimace grew. "Back then, there wasn't any protection for supernaturals. He ended up in an insane asylum and had to be rescued by oreads. Oreads were so spread out back then, it was two years before we realized he was in there. I was part of the rescue operation."

I swallowed hard. "Oh, gods."

Addie Beaumont glanced down at me. "This isn't two hundred

years ago, and we're in Havenwood Falls. But," she turned to Mom, "she probably does need someone to watch her while she sleeps. Or maybe find a way to take some precautions. We'll look into some spells that may help."

I rose off the floor. "I'm not sure I'm sleepwalking."

Addie met my gaze. "We've done everything we can for tonight. We'll look into some oread history and helpful spells, but for now, make sure you show up to clean off the graffiti and be extra cautious during the evening hours. We haven't found anything that makes us think you're dangerous."

I started to protest.

Mom stepped between us. "Thank you. I'm sorry you had to come out so late. Can we offer you anything to drink? Eat?"

"Thanks, but no." Addie moved toward the foyer and the door. "We'll be in touch."

She left.

Leda whistled. "Well, I don't think this family has had this much excitement in years."

Dad had been oddly quiet during the entire exchange, the agitation I'd seen in him when he stormed off the couch now a palpable glint in his eyes.

Mom must have noticed the same thing, because she approached him warily. "Honey, are you okay?"

Dad shook himself. "You know, I think I'm going to go in to work early today." His voice was sugary-sweet and entirely too cheerful, even mechanical. And his words were completely unexpected. He wanted to go in to work in the middle of the night?

Leda's gaze shot to the clock on our mantle. "At two o'clock in the morning?"

Dad sprinted for the stairs. "Yes, I do believe so. There's something I want to check on."

We stared after him. Never had I ever seen my dad act like that before. Normally, he was the calm one. Mom jumped, and Dad held her back. Perfect relationship. And now he was trying to escape?

Tears clogged my throat. "Is he that upset?" I asked, my voice small and strained.

Leda and Mom shared a look.

"I'll go in to work, too," Leda said. "And keep an eye on him."

This was wrong. Everything about this was wrong, and it was all my fault.

"I think I'm going to go take a shower," I whispered.

Mom closed her eyes, worry and strain lining her lips. "It's going to be okay, sweetie."

She knew the shower was an excuse for me to cry, but she didn't stop me or try to comfort me when I left.

Inside my bathroom, I turned on the faucet, letting the water run down the drain before sliding down the closed door outside the shower stall. Completely clothed. When I was upset, I didn't actually climb into the tub. I used the shower as an excuse and the sound of running water to drown out any sobs.

Pulling my cell phone out, I clicked on Jack's name in my contact list. "Please let it go through," I whispered. "Please."

Phone service in Havenwood Falls wasn't guaranteed. I wasn't sure if that had something to do with the mountains or the Court.

"Hello?" Jack's voice came over the line, deeper over the phone than it was in person. "Cressida?" Music played in the background, along with shouts I couldn't make out. "Shit," Jack swore, "hold on, don't hang up." Static sounded over the line. Rustling, and then, "When you have to get into a dead blasted closet just to hear something," he grumbled. "Cressida?"

I hiccupped, the tears I'd been holding back flooding out in massive, unladylike sobs. Snot, sniffling, and all. Minutes passed, my crying so hard, I'm pretty sure I gave up on breathing at some point.

"Hey," Jack said quietly, finally breaking through the emotional maelstrom. "If it makes you feel better, I'm on a first-name basis with the entire Havenwood Falls police department. Pretty sure my brother isn't far behind me. Let's just say, fourteen sucks for hellhounds."

I laugh-cried, which ended up sounding like something between a squealing brake and a dying animal.

"What did they get you for?" Jack asked.

"Destruction of property," I answered on a hiccup. "They said I spray-painted two buildings in Miller's Plaza." Another hiccup. "The charges were dropped, but," sniff, "I have to clean up the mess in a few hours."

Jack went quiet, and then, "No formal review?"

From that response, I knew he'd seen his fair share of the Havenwood Falls justice system.

"They still suspect sleepwalking. There was a similar case with an oread two hundred years ago. Well, not similar. The guy didn't commit crimes or anything, but—"

"Stay on track, darlin'. What are they doing about you?"

The *darlin'* made me pause. Was he even aware he'd said it?

"They're going to look into some spells. Otherwise, be extra vigilant at night and have someone watch when or if I sleep."

"That's a good start."

I lowered my voice. "I don't think I'm sleepwalking."

Something felt off about the way I "woke" up. As if I was a puppet whose strings had just been released.

"I believe you," Jack said. He'd said something similar before, but his faith in me felt even more important now.

"Why?"

"Because you snapped out of that shit too quick in the cemetery, and your behavior while out of it was . . . off. It looked more like a case of midnight schizophrenia than sleepwalking. You were a completely different person."

"How do you mean?"

"You were cruel. Well, cruel for *you* anyway."

His words rendered me speechless, the silence long and painful.

"It wasn't you," Jack said finally. "I don't have to know you all that well to recognize that. Call it intuition. And . . . it was your eyes. One moment you were affected by my hellhound gaze, and the next you weren't."

I sighed. The sound must have carried over the line because he added, "The scariest things are the things you can't see. The worst villains are the ones you can't detect."

"That sounded smart, Peters."

"That's because I am smart."

The almost hurt way he said it made me clutch the phone. "I didn't mean—"

"Don't sweat it. I get that a lot."

"No, but I really didn't mean—"

"I know." He chuckled. "I know you didn't mean it that way. Not coming from you anyway. It's fine. Really. "

"Good."

"Now, go. Try to relax, and feel free to . . . well, call me anytime."

My heart stuttered. "Okay."

"When the service works, that is," he added with a chuckle, the sound lightening the mood.

"Same," I replied. "I mean, you can call me anytime, too."

"Goodnight, Manos."

The call ended, and I stared at the phone, the water still running in the background.

CHAPTER 14

JACK PETERS

*M*idmorning found me in the shopping center on the south side of Main Street holding a grape soda and a coffee, my hip propped against a lamppost, my gaze on the small redhead sitting cross-legged on the warm sidewalk before VIP Nails. Her hair was a crazy mass of tied-up curls, her over-large T-shirt resting over blue-jeans shorts that looked like they'd been washed so many times the seams were in danger of popping. Buckets of soapy water with large sponges submerged in the murky depths sat next to her. Earbuds dangled from her ears, her gaze focused on the crazy artwork before her.

It was the crazy artwork that got to me.

My face broke out in a grin, my gaze traveling over the giant emojis Cressida had spray-painted all over the glass VIP Nails storefront as well as Long & Associates CPA. Everything from a smile emoji to a crying emoji to the classic poop one. Cressida's sinister alter ego had a sense of humor.

Pedestrians walked past, many of them stopping to stare as Cressida vigorously attacked the graffiti, their whispers loud and harsh. Things like "isn't that Wieland Manos's daughter" and "I heard she was seen at the police station with the Peters boy" and "Irene Beckett saw her cozying up to Jack Peters next to Coffee Haven" and "what a shame." Gossip in a small town could be brutal. Anger burned low and deep inside me, the hellhound caged within wanting nothing more than to stop the rumors coming her way. She didn't deserve them the same way my family did.

Closing the distance between us, I glared at the gawkers, seriously tempted to remove the sunglasses on my face. Hell, even with the glasses on, most of them scattered, recognition lighting their eyes with fear. The beast in me loved it.

Placing the drinks I brought on the sidewalk, I crouched next to Cressida, pulled one of her earbuds free, and nodded at the graffiti. "Couldn't the Mr. Hyde part of you be a little more creative?"

She jumped, her cheeks turning bright red. "I'm mortified. Absolutely mortified."

I laughed, pushing the biodegradable cup toward her. "Maybe this will help. Caramel macchiato, extra syrup. Willow said it was your regular."

She stared at me, a complicated rainbow of emotions lighting her eyes. "Why are you here?"

The question felt timid, as if the ugly snot crying she'd done on the phone with me the night before should have scared me away. If anything, it had drawn me closer to her. People didn't open up to me like that. Because of my reputation, people didn't trust me. She had.

Grabbing the grape soda, I twisted off the lid, took a quick swig, and then set it aside to submerge my hand in one of the buckets. "I needed the exercise." The sponge splatted against the store window, soap running down the glass in colored trails. "This shit is supposed to be good for fighting, right?" Swiping the sponge to the right, I parodied, "Wax on," to the left, "wax off."

Cressida's laugh rang through the still morning like tinkling bells, her shoulder nudging me. "I don't think I'm supposed to have any help."

Following her gaze, I glanced up to find Dao Pham, the owner of VIP Nails, glaring down at us, her face surrounded by dark hair with streaks of neon red. Covered in tattoos that highlighted her muscled arms, she cocked a brow, her leather-encased legs ending in a pair of stiletto heels that tapped impatiently. Dao had the kind of personality I related to—guarded and full of secrets. The story of my life.

I winked at her, even though I knew she couldn't see it, and then dropped my gaze. "Don't worry. I'd love to be a fly on the wall if she calls this in. The Kasuns will be too impressed I'm doing community service without getting charged with something first."

The earbud that had been in her right ear dangled between us, and I scooped it up, placing it awkwardly in my left ear canal.

Cressida tried to take it back, but I covered it with my hand and leaned away, the song Fall for You by Secondhand Serenade playing in my ear. "Not my usual taste in music, but it's not bad." The only reason I knew the song was because I'd been around too many girls who did like it.

She punched my shoulder. "Whatever."

Silence fell between us, an orchestra of noises surrounding us: music, splashing water, foot traffic, and passing vehicles. Unlike the places Pops used to take us riding during the summers, it didn't get hot enough in Havenwood Falls for the streets to get that melting blacktop smell. The greasy aroma of burgers and fries wafted from the Burger Bar nearby, the grill and fryer heating for the day ahead.

Cressida swiped at the store's glass, throwing occasional surreptitious glances my way. Our shoulders met, and even though the sleeves of our shirts kept our flesh from touching, I found myself distracted by her nearness.

We took too long working on the same part of the wall, her playlist flipping from song to song, my knees bumping hers, our hands running into each other as we cleaned, soap running everywhere.

The day grew warmer, the sun moving higher in the sky, and even though I could have spent today doing other things, I was glad it was this.

Touching the earbud in my ear, I ducked my chin. "You should add—"

A squeak interrupted me, a shadow falling over the two of us, and Cressida shot to her feet, the earbuds popping out of our ears to land on the cement, her phone clattering to the ground after it.

A beautiful tall dark-skinned girl, the same one who'd been at the Apex studio the weekend I'd helped deliver art supplies, stared at us, her mouth agape. Wearing a loose green summer dress that fell to her knees, she clutched a book to her chest like a shield.

"Hey." Cressida smoothed her hands down her damp, wrinkled shirt. "I tried calling you."

The girl's gaze traveled over the storefront before us, lines forming between her eyebrows. "So, it's true? You really graffitied Miller's Plaza?"

Cressida winced. "Well, not all of Miller's Plaza, and I didn't . . ." Her words trailed off. She'd been about to defend herself, but it didn't take a strong-nosed supe or heightened abilities to sense this girl was human. There wasn't a single explanation Cressida could give in her defense that didn't reveal a supernatural connection.

"It was my fault." Standing, I shoved my hands into my jeans pockets. "She took the fall for me."

Cressida's gaze flew to my face, but I simply offered her friend a wry, unapologetic smile. I hoped the rumor got around that I'd been the perpetrator. It was something people were more likely to believe, and Cressida was the type of person who would take the fall for someone. "I certainly didn't need anything else added to my rap sheet. She's my damsel in shining armor."

If I hadn't been wearing my sunglasses, Cressida would have seen the glint in my eyes daring her to protest. Human or no, I could tell Cressida was extremely close to this girl. Which meant caring about what she thought.

"Jack Peters, right?" the girl asked, shyly.

"Last time I checked. And you?"

"Paris Callahan." She gestured at Cressida. "We're best friends," and then, as if she needed to elaborate, "since elementary school."

"Oh." Damn. Color me impressed. Shocked, I swung my gaze between them. Only the supernaturals in Havenwood Falls would understand how hard it was to remain close friends with a human for so long. It was often difficult to hide what we were capable of, especially during puberty. Really sucky things tended to happen during puberty. And then, because of a memory ward placed on the town, there was the risk of forgetting where you came from if you left Havenwood Falls for too long. Whether it be family emergency or vacation. The same risk applied to supes, but because we were aware of the wards, it was more common among the humans. Humans didn't know to return within a certain timeframe.

Paris clutched her book so tightly the cover bent, her gaze taking in the scene. "Can I help?"

"No," Cressida yelped, and then backtracked, her gaze filling with concern. "Not that I don't want you to. It's just if you get too hot or . . ." Her words trailed off again, and I got the distinct feeling that whatever she was about to say wasn't supposed to be shared. This friendship was complicated.

Paris took pity on her. "I have diabetes," she admitted. "In its severest form. They're talking about getting me a pump. So," she shrugged, "I'm not supposed to overdo it."

Cressida glared. "Why'd you tell him that?"

It was one of the perks and one of the cons of being a hellhound. For some reason, humans found it easy to share their woes with me. This was great when doing business—Pops tended to abuse the power quite a bit—but it also made for really depressing conversations.

"Don't worry about it." I tapped her book. "What do you have there?'

Paris grinned. "A crossword puzzle. Well, kind of. This one's a little different. It gives you a trivia question rather than a word clue, and then you have to fill in the blocks with the answer."

"Why don't you sit and read them aloud while we work?" Cressida suggested.

"Really?" Paris chirped, her gaze swinging to my face. For a human, she was tall, just under six foot. "You okay with that?"

"Sure."

We returned to the buckets and sponges while Paris lounged in a small bit of shade near the building. Flipping the book's front cover open, she folded it under the back.

Time stood still, a comfortable easiness linking us.

Scrubbing the wall, I found myself glancing at Cressida, watching as she listened to Paris, her occasional laughter transforming her face. She reminded me of the stars my mother treasured so much, bright and engaging, yet so small. As if touching her would cause an explosion.

I'd had a lot of flings in my seventeen years, having gotten my first kiss at twelve and losing my virginity at fifteen, but I'd never considered a relationship. Especially with someone other than a hellhound. It took a strong woman to commit to our kind. Dating, sex, and marriage was one thing, having children another. Hellhound births were a risky business. Our species had a very high rate of deaths in childbirth. My mother passed away a year after my younger brother was born, her body unable to completely recover from the ordeal. She'd already challenged death twice by giving birth to me and my older brother. Most hellhound families had two children at best. Anything more was pushing the envelope.

Looking at Cressida now, it was hard to imagine a future like that for her. For anyone. It was why I remained single, even in high school. The thought threw a shadow over the afternoon.

"I'd better go," I said, dropping the sponge in the bucket.

Cressida looked at me, forehead creasing.

"I've got to do some delivery runs for Cerberus," I explained. It wasn't a lie. The company could use the extra hand, especially on the loading dock, but it wasn't something I *had* to do.

If she felt the change in mood, Cressida didn't acknowledge it, a smile forming on her lips and her gaze raking over my features. Almost as if she was memorizing my face before whispering, "Thanks for everything."

"Sure thing. Later."

Paris and Cressida returned to their conversation, and I hurried to my bike. The girl rattled me like no other girl had before.

What was I thinking?

I beat my chest with my fist, damning the beast. Hellhounds were different from other shapeshifters. Even though the beast within was part of us, there were times when it felt like it was its own sentient being, separate from our human bodies. Yet, despite how complicated it felt, it was also easier to control, the change dictated by us rather than a lunar cycle or other stimulants. A hellhound never shifted on a whim. If we shifted, we did it because we intended to kill. I'd never shifted, and I hoped I never had a reason to.

CHAPTER 15

CRESSIDA MANOS

I watched Jack leave with a growing sense of trepidation, the fear his nearness had kept at bay returning stronger than ever.

"What's going on with you and Jack Peters?" Paris asked, her knowing gaze catching mine. "Looks like a lot happened in a couple of days."

There were so many things I wanted to tell her, so many feelings I didn't understand that I wanted to share. In many ways, our friendship was a one-sided affair. Everything I said was calculated, every word weighed.

"I like him," I admitted, because a simple confession was the safest confession, but it came nowhere close to touching the magnitude of emotions swirling inside of me. It wasn't just that Jack was attractive. There was something vulnerable about him beneath his dangerous veneer. He was a mythological figure created by conjecture and fueled by his solitary nature. I was the girl everyone friended but never wanted to party with. It was ironic, really. A bad boy people went to for trouble. The good girl people went to in order to avoid it.

I liked him. I liked him a lot.

What did I even know about hellhounds? Other than what my

father had told me, the stuff about their powers and their eyes being dangerous to humans and some supes. That was basic information, stuff any supe could find out. It didn't touch on the personal stuff. Were they allowed to date outside their species? Did he shift very often?

Blowing out a breath, I scrubbed the building harder, my mind occupied by physical labor and Paris's occasional trivia question. The two of us had never needed to fill silence with conversation to enjoy our time together, but for once, I wished I could spill every secret I had to her.

Just once.

By the time mid-afternoon rolled around, I'd managed to clean the remaining graffiti from VIP Nails and most of it from Long & Associates. Paris departed halfway through my progress on the CPA's office, and I took that opportunity to throw everything I had into the work, using my supernatural speed and strength when there wasn't anyone in view, my gaze flicking to the sky.

The closer it got to nightfall, the more nervous I became, my body tensing in fearful anticipation.

The CPA's office had closed by the time I completed the cleanup, shadows growing long and sinister along the asphalt. The wet sponge dropped with a splash into the bucket, and I popped my knuckles, arching my back before lifting the two pails.

I was almost to a drainage pipe when a hand closed over mine on one of the pail's handles.

A screech tore from my lungs, the sound stoppered by Jack's soothing tone in my ear. "It's getting late."

It was the only explanation he gave.

My body responded to him instantly, the anxiety I'd been feeling swallowed up by his presence. "Did you finish at the delivery company?"

"For now." He dumped the bucket he'd taken from me and started to reach for the second one.

I jerked it away. "I've got it."

He'd done enough, spending most of his day helping me clean, and I was grateful that he seemed compelled to watch out for me. Compared to that, the bucket was nothing.

"I want to." His insistence felt personal somehow, as if he was frustrated while trying not to feel frustrated.

Which made me frustrated. "I've got this."

He tried taking the bucket. "Look, Cressy, I—"

"Cressida," I corrected, yanking on the pail.

A loud crack broke through the air, the pail flying up, paint-stained water raining down, completely soaking me and splattering him. Sometimes being short sucked.

"Look what you did!" I sputtered.

"Me?"

I prepared myself for the verbal bashing I knew was coming, but it never came.

He inhaled instead, the sound so sharp, it practically cut the air. "Holy shit, you're not wearing a bra."

My gaze dropped to my shirt. My very white, very wet, and now very transparent shirt. "Holy crap!"

Bad dreams about showing up naked at school had nothing on unintentionally flashing one of the hottest guys in Havenwood Falls with my nonexistent chest.

Jack broke into a fit of coughs, his fingers running under his sunglasses to rub at his eyes.

"Why are you not wearing a bra?" he choked.

Arms crossing, I backed away from him, my cheeks flaming so hot they practically caught on fire. "It's not like I was planning to get wet in front of anyone or anything."

Oh, gods! Was I trying to ruin my life? Wrong choice of words. Very, *very* wrong choice of words. Oh, that made this worse. *So* much worse.

Jack yanked the sunglasses off of his face, his eyes searching the empty street before his stunned gaze met mine. "Why are you not wearing a bra?"

The way he said it, all disapproval and no finesse, deepened my embarrassment and my anger. Why was he still stuck on this? "You saw! I don't exactly need a bra. So, could you please drop it."

"Yes, you do!" he argued, framing my chest with his hands despite my arms guarding them. "Those are at least an A, and the last time I checked, small boobs are still boobs, Manos!"

"Oh, no, you didn't," I groaned. "No, no you didn't!"

"Sheesh!" Shaking his leather cut off his shoulders, Jack offered it to me. His undershirt was as white as mine and completely useless as a cover-up, the wet fabric revealing a massive tattoo on his chest.

I pushed my arms through the cut, turning to protect whatever dignity I had left, my fingers pinching the leather closed over my breasts.

"Dear God, Manos," Jack muttered. "I hope you know what I just did for you. Whether it has patches or no, a biker doesn't give up his cut to anyone."

I wasn't sure how to respond to that.

He tugged me toward him, wrapping a protective arm around my shoulders. "Look, the clubhouse is closer. Let's get you one of my shirts, and then I'll see you home." We moved together, making it only a few steps when he added, "Start wearing a bra!"

"Oh, get over it already!" Anger born from serious mortification rose up like a fire-breathing dragon within me. "You can't tell me—"

"Start wearing one," he roared, cutting me off. "Because now every time I see you, I'm going to wonder if you have one on, and it's going to drive me insane."

His words stunned me into silence.

Replacing his sunglasses, he grumbled, "Small boobs are still boobs."

Sudden, unexpected laughter poured out of me, so hard and so fast I found it hard to breathe, tears dripping down my cheeks. As if my body needed the humor. Considering this had to be the craziest moment ever, maybe it did. How the devil did I manage to have my boobs looked at before I'd even gotten my first kiss?

"Thank you," I wheezed.

"What the hell?" Jack shook me. "Don't thank me! Why are you thanking me?"

I nudged him, almost affectionately. "Because your reaction is making me feel like a goddess. That's a big deal, Peters. I mean, have you seen me?"

"I see you. Trust me, I'm looking right at you."

Happiness, deep and joyful, washed over me, and—for a moment —I forgot to be afraid of the dark. I was already in deep, so why not go all the way? "You're going to fall in love with me."

Jack laughed incredulously. "Are you listening to yourself right now?"

I snuggled next to him, which was a complicated feat considering our height difference and the fact that we were walking. "I'm not wrong. Just wait and see."

"Is this a one-sided, unrequited thing?" he asked. "Or are you supposed to fall in love with me, too?"

"One-sided. I like the idea of you sitting in your room all solemn and love-piney. Maybe making those tiny little paper hearts, so you can throw them like flower petals on your floor while chanting, 'she loves me, she loves me not.'"

"Love-piney? You're unstable, you know that, right? What kind of crap is that? I find out you don't wear bras, and suddenly I'm going to fall in love with you. You are one strange girl, Cressida Manos."

Leading me to the motorcycle he'd parked on the street, he climbed on, patting the seat behind him.

I didn't hesitate. One, because I'd always wanted to ride a motorcycle, and two, because I was already in this deeper than I'd ever planned to be.

It wasn't until I'd settled behind Jack that I realized what a mistake riding with him was. He seemed to come to the same conclusion, because the next words out of his mouth were, "Just hold on and don't think about it."

Wrapping my arms around his waist, I plastered myself to him, shutting my eyes as tightly as I possibly could. Yep, all dignity gone.

He sped toward the MC clubhouse, my soaked chest against his damp back, and even though we weren't technically naked and I had the added protection of his cut, it certainly felt like we were skin-to-skin. His flesh was hot, a little too warm against me, but not hot enough to burn. I hoped.

Turning my head, I pressed my ear against his back, listening as his heart thudded, strong and steady. The bike rumbled beneath us, tying the sound of the road to his heartbeat, and I suddenly understood what he loved about the ride. All of it together, his heartbeat and the sound of the bike, sounded like a poem would read, smooth and lyrical. Wind rushed against us, Jack's skin a heater against the chill.

We pulled up to the clubhouse sooner than I expected, the gravel crunching under Jack's tires, and I pressed my nose into his back, hiding, because the only thing that could make this experience more mortifying would be parading past a clubhouse full of bikers, boobs flashing in a leather cut I shouldn't have on.

Way to win the family over.

"You're in luck. No one's here," Jack said, amused. "Pops had a run tonight, and Cade's with a friend. It'll be a few hours before anyone comes back here. It isn't often the clubhouse is empty like this. There's almost always someone here. Tonight, the universe is working for you."

Parking, he slipped off the bike and offered me his hand, pulling the cut closed for me as he helped me off the seat. "I'm going to warn you—this place isn't for the faint of heart."

The front room was dark when we entered, the only lighting neon beer lights and a stained-glass orb hanging above a full-length bar. The smell of cigarettes and beer permeated the air, a testament to excess. A sagging couch and jukebox were pushed up against a wall on the side of the room, overlooking a space occupied by a pool table and extra seating.

Jack rushed me past the clubroom, tugging me into a hallway full of doorways, most of them shut. He stopped in front of the last one on the left.

"No judgment," he insisted, pushing the door open.

Chaos met my gaze, my eyes falling on books, magazines, movies, a collection of knives, and soda bottles full of change. Half-naked women adorned his walls, and I hugged myself tight, completely aware that I lacked most of what they were flaunting.

Pulling his sunglasses off, Jack's gaze followed mine, and he promptly ripped three of the posters off the wall.

"Gifts," he said quickly. "All of them. The club members gave them to me."

To lessen the awkwardness, I leaned against a desk with a broken shelf and squinted at the titles on it. "You like history?"

Pulling a closet open, Jack yanked two shirts off the wire hangers inside with a clang, offering one of them—a black one—to me. "I like the feeling I get when I study it. As if I'm standing on a battlefield or exploring places no one else has seen, and even though those things have already happened, there's so much more we can learn from the literature and artifacts people have left behind."

"So, it's human history that interests you?"

"Both. Though human history is less complicated."

"You should talk to my parents. My dad's over six hundred years old. He actually lived in France during the revolution."

"Holy shit!" Jack's eyes lit up. "Really?"

I laughed. "It's less exciting if you've heard the stories as much as I have."

"Try drunk history lessons about Blackbeard the pirate."

"Your Pops?" Turning away from him, I dropped his cut onto the bed, and then removed the wet T-shirt. At this point, I didn't care if he saw my bare back. My back was a whole lot less embarrassing than my front. I think everyone had at least one feature they'd like to change. I didn't think I was ugly. I actually liked my looks a lot, but I still hoped my chest went up at least one cup size. Then again, maybe not. I liked going braless.

"Six hundred years . . ." Jack cleared his throat. "So, you'll live a long time, too?"

"I could. It's not that oreads can't die; it's just that we're harder to kill. We don't catch human illnesses, and we won't die from a fall. We get wounded like humans do, though. We can be shot, stabbed, scratched, and so forth. We just heal from the wounds. Some wounds take longer than others to go away, but we can usually heal from them." I turned to face him. "We have the potential to live a very, very long time."

Jack's expression grew thoughtful. "Hellhounds, too. I mean, obviously, if Pops met Blackbeard. Pops is over three hundred years old. Male hellhounds tend to live longer than the females."

Jack pulled his wet shirt over his head, leaving his chest bare, and I completely lost the ability to follow along with our conversation. Tattoos covered his skin, accentuating his muscles. A chain wrapped one bicep while a skull and compass covered the other, but neither of those held a candle to the masterpiece on his chest. A three-headed beast was tattooed across his broad torso, each head with a gaping mouth holding different objects. The first head bit down on a cracked tombstone with no epitaph written on it. The second was impaled by a tree of life, the branches wrapping around its spiky head, the roots growing into its jaw. And the third held a ship with full sails, its mouth full of choppy waves.

I suddenly found it hard to breathe because something told me Jack had chosen this tattoo for extremely personal reasons.

"You should put that back on," I said, shoving his shirt back at him, and then dropping it when I realized it was the wet one.

"What?" Jack asked, amused. "Have you never seen a man's chest before?"

Not one like his. Most definitely not one like his.

"Or here, put this one on." I shoved the dry shirt he'd pulled out of the closet at him. Even going so far as to try putting it on for him. "Just, you know, back on. Like a good—"

"If you say 'good boy' like I'm some well-trained show dog, I'm going to throttle you." Taking the shirt from me, he draped it over my head and left it there, the fabric hanging in my face.

I yanked it off, letting it fall to the floor. "Aren't you, technically, a dog?"

"Not funny, Manos. Not even close to being funny."

"Yes, huh. Admit it." I pinched my fingers together and held them up. "It was a little funny. Just a little."

He glared.

I pinched my fingers even closer together. "A wee tiny bit."

He jerked me toward him, and I squealed as his large hand cupped my waist. The red hue in his eyes flared, his gaze dropping to my lips.

"Oh," I whispered. "You're not . . . I mean you're not going to, uh, kiss me, are you?"

"Cressida?"

"Yeah?"

"Shut up."

His lips fell on mine, the gentle way he kissed stealing any thoughts I had about stopping him. He tasted like the grape soda he seemed so fond of—if the change bottles on the floor were any indication—his tongue touching mine. I sighed, letting him take the lead, my body relaxing into his. Time slowed, his lips and tongue testing, nipping, and soothing mine, sending tingles of sensation zipping through my body.

His head rose, his gaze searching mine. "What the hell am I going to do with you?" he whispered. "You're too small to get under my skin the way you do."

The words startled me, and I placed a hand against his chest, my palm splayed over the tree-impaled beast head. "For a first kiss, that wasn't bad at all. I think my heart hurts."

As if he'd been burned, Jack released me, and I stumbled toward his bed. "Oh, darlin', we definitely shouldn't be doing this." Leaning down, he swiped his shirt off the floor and tugged it over his head, the fabric swallowing the beasts on him. "Come on, let me get you home before I do something I regret."

As I followed him out the door, the illogical part of me, the insane inner Cressida, couldn't help but wonder what being a regret would feel like.

CHAPTER 16

JACK PETERS

I knew by the way Cressida tensed behind me that something was wrong when I pulled up to her house, her reaction completely wiping clean the conflicted thoughts I'd been having on the drive over. The Manos place was the perfect example of a mountain home—stone and wood with a wraparound porch, two chimneys, and a line of inviting rocking chairs overlooking the mountain. The windows blazed with light from the second story down.

As soon as I cut the engine, I took Cressida's hand in mine, slipping it off my waist before cradling it in my palm. "What is it?"

"All the lights are on."

I glanced back at her. "That's not normal?"

"What time is it?"

Fishing my phone out of my pocket, I clicked on the backlight. "After eleven." We'd been riding for a while after we left the clubhouse. I hadn't wanted to take her directly home, and she hadn't stopped me. Her embrace during the ride had felt good. Comforting.

Cressida tugged on her ear while worrying her lip with her teeth. "I don't guess it's abnormal. But mom knew I'd be out because of the cleanup, so she wouldn't have waited up. And Dad's usually in his office after dinner, but the car's not here." She stared at the windows.

"Mom's really into conserving electricity when she can. I don't know . . . something doesn't feel right. Every single light is on."

Slipping off my bike, I forced her behind me and preceded her to the door. "I'll check it out first."

"No!" She grabbed me by the arm. "You can't! If nothing's wrong, how do I explain you crashing into my house? They don't even know I'm with you."

"Fine, then we go together," I stated firmly. I wasn't taking no for an answer.

She frowned, her hand closing over mine on the door knob. I fisted my free hand, lifting one finger, then two, then three.

We burst through the opening, the light in the foyer hitting us in the face. Beautiful Persian rugs lined polished hardwood floors that reflected fine crystal chandeliers, the front room leading to a living area on the left, a kitchen on the right, and a staircase down the center.

"Mom?" Cressida stepped forward cautiously, her heart beating so loudly, I could hear it in my ears, the smell of her fear strong in my nostrils. The hair on my arms stood up, the beast in me crouching, muscles bunched.

Footsteps pounded on the stairs, startling us. A frantic, barefoot, auburn-haired woman stepped onto the landing, running past us into the kitchen. Theia Manos.

"Mom?" Cressida followed her. "What's wrong?"

She didn't spare us a glance. "I hate that cat. Hate it! Do you hear me? Hate it! Where did you put it, you lousy little feline?"

Theia rushed through the kitchen, forcefully slamming drawers and yanking open cabinets, her body a flurry of madness, her movements violent.

"Mom!" Cressida's voice rose. "What's wrong?"

The woman's head shot up, her unfocused gaze landing on her daughter. Pure evil stared back at us. "Ah! You! You, you, you, you, you! Do you have any idea what your cat has done?"

I'd seen this look before, back when I'd caught Cressida in the cemetery. Only her mother's stare was a lot more brazen, a lot more cruel.

"Slink?" Cressida's voice shook, and I gripped her arms with my hands, steadying her.

Theia growled. "That cat's been dropping my jewelry into the toilet! The toilet! Why the hell would she drop my jewels into the toilet?"

"What? Mom, Slink doesn't mess with jewelry. Just suits and shoes."

"Then where is it!" Theia shouted. "Where the hell is it! She took it from me!"

Cressida stumbled into me, a whimper rushing past her lips, my arms becoming a vise around her. My beast roared.

Theia laughed, the sound hollow and eerie, before streaking out of the room, her movements so fast, I barely saw her brush past me, even with my hellhound abilities.

"Mom!" Cressida panicked, spinning to face me. "That's not my mother."

She didn't have to tell me that. "I know."

The sound of a cat yowling filled the house, pitiful and loud. Desperate. Like screams heard just before someone or something died.

Cressida screamed. "Oh, my gods! She's killing my cat."

Grabbing her hand, I yanked Cressida toward the stairs, following the cat's screeching, panicked adrenaline feeding the beast inside me. He snarled, pacing.

We found them in an upstairs pastel blue bathroom, her mother kneeling on a fuzzy bathroom rug, her hands shoving a tortoise-hair cat into the toilet, its head down. Over and over again. "Find my jewelry, you despicable beast!"

The cat fought for its life, clawing for purchase, its nails lacerating the skin and drawing blood on Theia's arms.

"Mom!" Cressida threw herself at them, tackling her mother against the tub.

The cat fell, water flying from its wet fur, its entire body trembling. I tried approaching it, but it hissed, blurring past me into the rooms beyond. Cats and hellhounds didn't mix. I hadn't met one yet that liked me, even when I was trying to save it.

Gripping her by the arms, Cressida shook her mother, repeatedly. "Mom!"

Theia fought her, her clawed-up hands going for Cressida's throat.

"Watch out!" I yelled.

The beast in me leapt, and I doubled over, taking slow, deep breaths to avoid shifting. If I shifted now, someone was dying.

Cressida flung herself to the side, ducking down just as her mother's hands closed over the spot where'd she been.

Sobbing, Cressida sat up, her expression resolved. "Oh, Mom. I'm so sorry."

The words rang through the bathroom, the apology a precursor to the slap she suddenly gave her mother across the face, the force of it sending Theia reeling into the bathtub, the apology hanging heavy in the air.

Silence fell.

Downstairs a door slammed open. "Mom! Cressida!"

Cressida scrambled to her feet. "Leda!"

Feet pounded on the stairs, and a harried, blond-haired woman in a wrinkled black business suit ducked into the room, stopping short when she caught sight of the scene before her. "Oh, my gods!"

Theia groaned. "Leda? Cressida?" She pushed herself up against the tub, leaving a faint trail of blood behind her. "What's going on?" She shook her head, blinked, and then glanced at her arms. "What is this?" Troubled eyes slid to Cressida. "Did you do this?"

"What? Mom, no!" Cressida objected.

Leda gasped, supporting herself on the doorframe, her astonished gaze finding her sister's face.

The horror of the situation suddenly dawned on me. Cressida had committed several minor crimes in the middle of the night, first by painting a tombstone, then by tagging two buildings. As far as her family was concerned, whatever strange ailment she seemed to have *only* affected her. Theia had apparently forgotten what she'd just done. It was the same thing that had been happening to her daughter.

Cressida's mouth fell open. "No," she gestured at me, her eyes full of desperation. "I've been in town cleaning graffiti. We just got here.

All the lights were on when we came in." Her gaze shot to Theia. "Mom was running around the house, yelling something about my cat and jewelry. Then she tried to drown Slink." Eyes pleading, she touched the claw marks on her mother's arm gently. "Slink did that, Mom. I didn't do this. I swear! You were trying to kill Slink."

It was way past time for me to step in. "Cressida's right, Mrs. Manos. You weren't acting right when we arrived. I've seen that same crazed look before—in the cemetery, on your daughter's face. We need to figure out what's going on here."

Leda's blue-eyed gaze shot to my face. "We? What do you have to do with any of this?"

"Stop it!" Cressida warned. "He helped me. Not once. Not twice. Not three times. More than that. I told you," her gaze glanced off the faces in the room, "something is wrong here. I told you!"

"Let's just everyone calm down," Theia mumbled weakly. "Where's your dad?"

"I don't know," Leda said. "That's why I'm here. We were at work, and then he was just gone."

Theia tried to stand, but slipped in the blood. I caught her, my muscles bunching. "We need to contact the Court," she breathed against my shirt. "If what you're saying is true, Cressida, then whatever is causing this is somehow undetectable. First you, then me and your dad . . ."

We moved out of the bathroom, Leda and Cressida in the lead while Theia leaned on me for support.

"Do you remember what you did?" I asked Theia.

She shook her head.

"What about before? Did you fall asleep earlier?"

"No, I don't think so." She frowned.

A terrible feeling bloomed in my chest. Wieland Manos was missing, and Theia Manos had gone mad while awake.

Ahead of me, Cressida turned. Her green eyes were unfocused, her pupils dilated.

Whatever this was haunting the Manos family no longer needed them to sleep.

"For the love of . . ." I shoved Theia at Leda. "Go! Take your mom! It's got Cressida!"

By some terrible twist of fate, I had to start falling for a girl who happened to be an oread.

Cressida took off, a blur in my peripheral vision as she tore past me. And there was the crux of my problem. Oreads were too damn fast.

"Shit!" I tore through the house after her, yanking open every door I came to, my thoughts flying back to the cemetery, to the first night Cressida had been possessed by whatever took hold of her now. That version of Cressida, the Mr. Hyde to her usual, fun-loving Jekyll, had been amused by me.

"That's it!" I shouted. "I'm going to spend the rest of my life feeding you the most decadent, richest foods I can find, so you become completely unable to run."

Laughter floated down the hall toward me, and I paused, listening.

"That's right," I murmured, following the sound. "Keep it up, you bastard." The beast in me jumped for joy, claws springing out. "Not tonight, hellhound," I soothed. "I really don't want to go down in history for eating my first girlfriend."

The laughter grew, high-pitched and unnatural, the sound leading me to a room at the end of the hall. I knew even before I entered that it belonged to Cressida. It smelled like paint and coconuts.

The door creaked when I pushed it, swinging open to reveal a simple room with a bed and white dresser on one side, a desk and full-length mirror on the other. Art work exploded on her walls, the space full of colorful canvases and shadowbox shelves holding sculptures and pottery.

But it wasn't the artwork I stared at now. It was Cressida.

She stood in front of her full-length mirror, a carpet of curly red hair laying at her feet, a pair of scissors clutched in her hand. The horror of it made me freeze. Whatever was inside Cressida didn't just want to make her do bad things—it wanted to hurt her, too. Every single time it inhabited her, it found a way to strike out. By alienating her, turning her into a criminal, and now this.

"Why?" I asked softly, ever so carefully edging my way forward. "Why do you do this? Every single time you take her, you find a way to hurt her. Why are you so dead set on hurting her?"

Cressida turned, her head cocking to the side, her hand fluffing the newly shorn ear-length curls. "Because of who she is."

I took another step forward. "And who would that be?"

Laughing, she twirled the scissors, fisting them in her hand before placing them against her neck.

My heart stuttered, the beast in me causing my skin to run hot.

"The backbone of her family," Cressida answered. The scissors inched forward.

I have never moved so fast in my life. In a blink, I was in front of her, my hand wrapped around hers on the scissors, the point just piercing the skin.

A drop of blood welled up on her neck, rolling like a tear down her collarbone.

"Let her go," I growled. Unfocused eyes peered into mine, and I used my shoulder to knock off my sunglasses. "Let her go." Cressida recoiled, my naked gaze holding hers. My eyes had worked before. Whatever this was, my gaze was its weakness. "Let her go."

Cressida slumped, her hand becoming limp, and I let the scissors fall to the floor, my arms catching her in my embrace.

"Jack," she whispered. This voice, this girl, was mine.

CHAPTER 17

CRESSIDA MANOS

"*I* know how to make it leave you alone."

Those were the first words I heard when I came to, my body draped in Jack's arms, his red-hued gaze on my face. "It happened again?"

"It can't handle looking into a hellhound's eyes," he replied.

We were in my bedroom, the art-covered walls a kaleidoscope of colors, all of it suddenly too bright and too much.

Letting my head fall, I started to turn my head, but Jack's hand stopped me. "Don't," he pleaded.

Somewhere in the house, my mother and sister called my name. My head felt light. *Too* light.

"What is it?" I whispered.

Jack looked away.

"Cressida!" My sister's voice rang out from the open doorway. I lifted my head, my gaze finding her weary face. My mother hung onto her for support.

One look at me, and Leda's eyes widened. "Oh, Cressida."

Mom gasped, her hand flying to her mouth.

Fear pricked my skin. "Jack," I whispered. "Is there something wrong with my face?"

Setting me down gently, Jack slid his arm around my waist, took my chin in his hand, and tilted my head toward the mirror.

A moment passed, my eyes adjusting to the image before me and the ear-length red curls that framed my face. The cut was crude, the bottom uneven. I looked like little orphan Annie. Only older.

"Oh, thank the gods!" I exclaimed when I finally found my voice. "I thought something had happened to my face!"

In the mirror beside me, Jack cracked up, his laughter deep and satisfying.

"Your hair!" Mom cried from the doorway.

I touched it tentatively. "Hair grows back. You can't grow back a face."

Jack's laughter grew. "I should have known." He hugged me from behind, his chin resting on the top of my head. "I should have known this wouldn't bother you."

Downstairs, a door slammed, completely shattering the moment.

"Dad!" Leda and I cried.

Jack rushed to the door, leaving me behind. "Stay with your mom and sister. If he's been taken by that thing, then he needs to look into my eyes."

Love is like a Band-Aid. Anything bad needs to be revealed straight from the get-go. Rip. Over. One thing the Manoses had never been good at was waiting. By pure luck—and because Mom and I were sucked dry of energy—Jack made it to the stairs first.

"Honey!" my dad shouted. "Cressida! Anyone home?"

We all looked at each other.

"He sounds okay," Leda hissed.

"Like he always does," Mom agreed.

None of that meant anything.

Jack took a step down. "I'm going in first."

My mother scowled. "And if he's not being possessed, you're going to give him a heart attack."

"I thought oreads couldn't die from human illnesses," Jack said smoothly.

Mom threw me a dirty look. "How long have you known this guy? And you're already spilling secrets."

I pouted. "You tried to kill my cat." Speaking of, where was Slink?

Jack rushed down the stairs, Leda on his heels. Mom and I moved much, much slower.

"Dad!" Leda called.

Wieland Thanos stepped into the foyer from the kitchen, confusion etching his brows. "Why are all the drawers and cabinets open in here?"

His gaze rose, his entire body freezing when he caught sight of Jack, a snarl curling his lips. Something moved in his eyes.

Jack tackled Dad before my father could make a move, his hands grasping Dad by the face.

"You can't have the jewel!" Dad screamed, his voice full of greed and desperation. "It's mine. Only mine!"

"Look at me!" Jack snarled, thrusting his nose against Dad's, eyes locked.

Thrashing twice, my father's body went limp.

Everything about the last week ran together like one of those melted crayon wax projects my mother used to help me do when I was a child—images and conversations bombarding me, with one important fact standing out the most.

Sagging on the stairs, my fingers gripped the rails, my warm, flushed face pressed against the wood.

"It's the delivery," I said, my gaze flashing to Jack's face. "The weekend delivery, the one you and your father brought to the store Saturday. The jewel dad bid on. This all started after we received the jewel. It has to be the jewel! That's what's causing this."

Jack released my father.

Dad slid to one of the Persian rugs on the floor, the red, black, and tan patterned carpet a part of Dad's collection of antique treasures. Considering Jack's love of history, I wondered how impressed he'd be if he knew the rug was an original, the piece dating back to the Safavid period.

Mom and Leda fell into a thoughtful silence, my words sitting heavily between us. It all made sense. Mom and Dad's strange tension-filled behavior, their odd argument, the sudden fascination with the emerald at work, Mom attempting to kill my cat over lost jewelry, and my father's jealous obsession. It all came back to the jewel.

Jack trotted up the stairs. "Would a jewel have that kind of power? Enough that even the Court couldn't detect it?"

Exhausted, he sat a step below me, his hand gripping the same rail my hand gripped, our fingers brushing. This night felt long, even if only a couple hours had passed, and now that we'd discovered the mysterious villain plaguing us couldn't hold a hellhound's gaze, Jack was being forced to play the longest game of "see who blinks first."

"We could check Dad's records at the store," I suggested.

Above me, Mom groaned, her injured arms cradled against her body.

A ball of dark fur tiptoed along the upstairs landing, slinking carefully down toward me, the cat curling into a shivering ball at my back. Slink avoided both my mother and Jack, her usual playfulness subdued.

The last week and this night had left mental and physical scars on all of us.

"We need to contact the Court," Leda said.

"Wait. I want to talk to my father first," Jack insisted. "He'll have records on the delivery, and some insight on the seller. Plus, if the jewel is the source of the problem, we'll have something to turn over to the Court. Until then, no one goes near the stone."

"I don't think staying away from it is the solution. I've never even seen it, and it's still affecting me." On a whim, I reached out, running my fingers through the top of Jack's hair. His eyes fell shut, the lines on his face smoothing.

Dad stirred below, his lanky body coiling as he pushed himself off the floor. His hair was a spiky mess, his navy-blue polo shirt was pulled haphazardly out of his slacks, and his pockets were turned inside out.

He peered up at us, his green eyes clouded with confusion. "I think I've misplaced something."

Tense and alert, Jack shot down the stairs. "Mr. Manos?"

"I'm pretty sure I've misplaced something." Pressing his fingers against his brow, Dad tapped it repeatedly. "It was right here just a moment ago."

Pulling herself up against the railing, Leda whispered, "Is he possessed?"

Jack peered into Dad's eyes. "No, I'm not getting anything."

My stomach ached, my hands clutching my abdomen. "The jewel has driven him mad."

A faint sob shook Mom's frame, a tear slipping down her cheek.

My heart broke. Oreads depended on family, on the tight bonds formed between us. It gave us strength. What was happening to us now tested that.

Jack fished his phone out of his jeans pocket before meeting my gaze. "Keep an eye on your dad. I'm going to go find my father. If something happens before I get back, slap whoever is affected. That seemed to work before with your mom in the bathroom."

"And if it doesn't?" I asked.

Jack frowned.

"We'll make it work," Leda promised. "Just go get your dad, biker boy. We need answers and help before this gets worse."

Jack's gaze found mine, concern flicking through his eyes, before he rushed out the door.

CHAPTER 18

JACK PETERS

*W*hen I returned to the clubhouse, it was no longer empty. Unconscious bodies littered the space, the forms sprawled across the floor, the threadbare sofa lining the wall, and the pool table resting in the center of the room. Half-naked women spooned with men in leather vests sporting a sword-impaled skull and patches. Empty beer bottles and specially mixed brews from Sanguine's Elixirs dripped sticky liquid onto scarred hardwood floors. Blood, alcohol, and God knew what else. I was suddenly glad Cressida and I had left when we did. More than likely, these guys had stumbled in from Silk after enjoying way too much alcohol. It wouldn't surprise me if Melaina had kicked them out. The members got rowdy when they got drunk.

The prospects were going to hate cleaning up the mess.

Anxiety over leaving Cressida and her family chased away all other thoughts, the apprehension eating at me as I picked my way around the bodies and walked toward a door at the back of the room, my stride full of purpose and determination.

I knew he was in there, and I knew he was awake. He always was.

The door made no sound when I opened it.

Inside the room, my father sat at a long mahogany table, his head bent over a stack of papers, his fingers twirling a knife. I watched it spin on the wood.

"Pops."

Liam Peters looked up, his hard gaze finding mine, the sunglasses he always wore pushed up on top of his head. The glasses held back his too-long sandy hair, his face covered in scruff. Tattoos lined his arms.

"Pops, I need your help."

Liam eased back in his chair, rolling it back, the seat creaking as he crossed his ankle over his knee, his hand resting on his leg. Waiting.

"There's an issue with one of the deliveries we made. I need some information on it," I said.

"Does this have anything to do with the Manos girl?"

I paused. "How did you know?"

"I've been watching you. And them."

I recoiled.

Amused by my reaction, Pops reached out to tap the papers on the meeting room table. "I didn't get the position I have at this club for nothing, son. It's my job to keep my ear to the wire. When I heard your girl had been arrested and that Addie Beaumont was looking into the oread problem, I did a little digging."

He pushed the papers my way.

I leaned over the table, thumbing through the top few documents. The arrest report for Cressida Manos, including a detailed monologue from Cressida claiming her innocence.

"Why?" I asked. Pops wasn't one to involve himself in Havenwood Falls drama, especially something as small as a sleepwalking incident.

"My first job is protecting you and your brothers. My beast knew something was wrong. If it involves my club or my family, it's my business," Liam said firmly. "And you wouldn't have helped the Manos girl clean graffiti in the middle of a shopping center if you weren't interested in pursuing something with her. You may not always like what I do for a living, son, but everything I do is for you, your brothers, and this brotherhood." He tapped his face. "I've got eyes everywhere."

"She's not sleepwalking."

"Keep reading," Liam prompted.

I flipped the pages over, revealing an account sheet, the file listing a wire transfer for funds to a man a few towns over. Belen Cirillo.

"That's the seller of the jewel Wieland Manos bid on," Pops informed me.

My head shot up, anger marring my features. "You know it's the jewel? Why didn't you say anything? Why didn't you *do* anything? Do you even know what that family has been through? This week and tonight?"

Pops threw me a warning look. "I wasn't a hundred percent positive until last night, and I only work with positives." He leaned forward. "That delivery gave me a bad feeling from the start. I would have investigated this even if you hadn't started taking an interest in Wieland's daughter. It didn't take a lot of deductive reasoning to realize it was after our delivery that things started going wrong for the Manos family."

We were running out of time. The jewel's power was getting stronger, the effects growing. It had gone from affecting Cressida in her sleep to driving Wieland Manos mad.

"What did you find out about the jewel?"

Pops stood, gathering the papers in his hands. "Let's discuss this with the Manos family. I can end this for them now. Tonight. Before it gets worse."

Being the son of Liam Peters wasn't easy. Pops was a known outlaw with a list of vices three hundred years long. People judged me based on his past and his present decisions, while also expecting me to take over for him in the future. At times, I hated it. But then there were times—like now—when I looked at my father, and I realized just how mighty he was, how easy it was for him to fix a problem the rest of us shed blood and tears over, with a simple stack of paperwork.

The beast in me growled, frustrated. I'd wanted a fight. I wanted to be a hero.

Pops squeezed my shoulder, sensing my anger. "The beast is always restless, son. It's just the way it is for hellhounds. But you listen to me, and you listen to me good. You don't release the beast until you're prepared to deal with the consequences. I've got a lot of blood on my hands. The longer I can keep that blood off your hands, the better. Some things are better resolved by paperwork and politics than violence. The difference between a good leader and a great one is knowing when to deal with things this way," he waved the papers at me, "or that way." His eyes flared, flames burning in their depths, and for a moment I caught a glimpse of the beast that was my father.

"Let's ride," he said.

CHAPTER 19

CRESSIDA MANOS

The healing claw marks on Mom's arms and hands had gone from angry and red to pink and bruised, the blood having crusted up as it dried. She hissed when I dabbed it with antiseptic, the skin still scratched enough to burn.

"I'm sorry," Mom said, her gaze raking over my face as I unrolled a ball of gauze. "I'm sorry I didn't listen to you."

"I'm not angry," I promised. "Truth is, I wouldn't have believed me either. No one sensed the magic, and there *are* past cases of sleepwalking oreads."

I started to wrap Mom's wounds, but she touched my face, stopping me. Honestly, the wounds wouldn't last long enough to need bandaging, but doing it made me feel better. "It doesn't matter. I should have trusted you. You've never given me any reason not to."

Tears welled up at the back of my eyes, and I blinked to keep them from falling.

Dropping her hand, Mom smiled gently. "Your father and I waited a very, very long time to have children, and it wasn't until we settled in Havenwood Falls that we were even sure we wanted any." Her gaze grew distant. "Lord, your father could be impulsive. When he bought the old Campbell's Market from Callum Campbell and told me he wanted to put a jewelry store in it, I thought he'd lost his mind. New town. New business. It was all so overwhelming, but it was opening Summit that led to having you girls, so it turned out to be the best decision we ever made."

Mom rambled, telling the same story I'd heard repeatedly over the years, the familiar tale soothing her frazzled nerves. In many ways, I was a lot like my mother. We rambled when we had nothing to say and grew quiet when we had too many words.

"I called in someone to help at the store," Leda said suddenly from the kitchen door.

I looked up from where I was sitting at the table. "How's Dad?"

"Not much better," Leda admitted, rubbing her eyes. "I should have known something was off. Things have been weird at the shop. Dad's been more spastic than usual. It's just . . . I've been distracted."

"Don't start blaming yourself," Mom told her. "You do that, and everything else around you will start falling apart. None of this is anyone's fault."

"Still." Leda tugged on her wrinkled blazer.

We all needed a change of clothes and a bath, but I was afraid to do anything until Jack returned.

Mom's gaze grew soft, a smile on her lips. "Falling in love is a complicated thing, isn't it? So small in the bigger scheme of things. But it feels so big when it's happening, as if the entire world revolves around one person and the moments you share with them."

Leda and I shared a look.

Mom snorted. "Oh, don't look at each other like I'm crazy. I've been watching the two of you, even through all this mess. I know you're both seeing someone. Or, at least," she glanced at me, "talking to someone."

Leda recoiled. "Let's focus on Cressida's relationship. She's the one seeing a biker."

"Oh, no!" I stood. "I see exactly what you're doing here. Using me to avoid your relationship woes."

"That's because we don't have a relationship."

We all froze.

"We?" I asked. "Ha!" I clapped my hands in triumph. "You just said we. There's potential there, or you wouldn't be protesting so much."

Gliding into the kitchen, Leda ruffled my short curls. "Did you kiss the biker yet? You two looked awful cozy on the stairs earlier. Very domestic."

"Oh, you!" I swatted at her.

"Does this mean we're supposed to call you his old lady now? Is that a thing?"

"I'm warning you . . ."

"Not that I'm against the whole leather look they've got going on. Have you seen the Melaina Savage woman?" My sister whistled.

"Leda!"

Mom smiled a tired, wistful smile. "I love you girls." An emotional silence, full of affection and amusement, washed over us.

A crash in the living room shattered the moment, and we rushed out of the kitchen, completely on edge.

Dad crawled on the floor toward us, dragging himself into the foyer, his body convulsing.

"It's going to kill me," he cried. Rolling over, he beat the back of his head against the floor and clawed at the Persian rugs, bunching the fabric in his hands. "It's going to kill me." His eyes rolled into the back of his head. "And then it's going to kill all of you."

A half-laugh, half-sob spewed from his lips, tears leaking from the corners of his eyes. His legs kicked violently, his head beat, beat, beating, until spots of blood appeared beneath him.

Leda rushed to his side, tears pouring down her face as she threw herself over his legs. I fell to my knees behind his head, my hands gripping his face, my arms straining desperately to hold him still.

"Stop, Dad!" Leda pleaded.

He screamed, the sound full of agony and despair, as if he was seeing the end of the world. "Dying," Dad whispered. "We're all going to die."

"Please make it stop," Mom begged, kneeling next to us. "Whatever this is, please make it stop. I can't stand it anymore."

The quickest way to defeat an oread was to defeat its family.

Dad screamed and screamed and screamed.

The door to the house flew open.

A hard-faced Liam Peters marched in, his sunglasses missing, his combat boots coming to a stop on our expensive Persian rugs, Jack on his heels. The hellhounds should have looked out of place in our formal foyer with their large statures, leather cuts, and massive builds, but Liam and Jack owned whatever space they entered.

"Get it together, Wieland," Liam commanded. He gestured for us to move away, and my sister and I backed up, letting the biker take our place.

With no finesse whatsoever, Liam grabbed Dad by the collar, lifted him up until they were eye to eye, and then growled, the sound coming from way deep down inside of him. His eyes flared, flames leaping in his pupils, his voice dangerously low when he demanded, "You asshole of a god, it takes a coward to fight the way you do. How about you do me a favor and pop out of the oread here?"

Dad's back arched.

Liam grinned, baring teeth that weren't quite human. "Release him!"

Dad slumped, his hands searching for purchase on Liam's arms. He gulped in breath, his face turning red. "You think you know how to defeat me, don't you?" Dad asked wearily.

Jack stepped forward. "You looked into his eyes, Pops. Why isn't—"

"You don't want to tangle with me, god," Liam warned.

"If it isn't them, it will be someone else. I'm never finished." Dad laughed weakly.

Liam shook him, lifting his chin so that his eyes rested on the hellhound's. "It's gods like you that give supernaturals a bad reputation."

Dad panted, visibly fighting against the hellhound's gaze. "Of course, his daughter would have to fall for one of you."

"Her lucky day, I guess," Liam retorted. His eyes flared, and Dad sagged in his embrace, as if whatever had possessed him had suddenly fallen out of him.

"Wieland!" Mom fell against them, her bandaged hands clinging to her husband, and Liam released him into her embrace. Mom hugged Dad to her. "Wieland."

His arms snaked around her waist.

"Okay," he gasped. "Okay, I'm okay." His eyes cleared, the pain that had been lining his face ebbing away. "Thank you." Together they scrambled to their feet. Dad shook, his body leaning on Mom for support. "What was that? What was in me?"

Unlike with Mom and me, Dad's memory seemed intact.

"Ancient Greek power at its best." Liam leaned against the foyer wall, arms crossed. "You really do know how to purchase jewelry, Manos."

Jack came to me, pulling me into his embrace, his arms falling around me. The move was a little showy for Jack, and I wondered if this had something to do with his dad.

Liam nodded at his son, a look passing between them.

"Goes to show that some things can be ended without violence." Pulling a rolled-up sheaf of papers out of his back pocket, Liam offered them to my father. "I need to confiscate the emerald you purchased from Belen Cirillo, whether I have to get it from here or from Summit."

Dad accepted the papers. "What's this?"

"This is about ending the tragedy in store for your family if you don't concede the jewel. Things are bad now, but they're only going to get worse if that emerald remains in your possession." Liam tapped the papers. "There's a copy of your sales receipt along with a certificate of authenticity the seller failed to give you. I'm having a tough time finding out where Belen got the jewel in the first place, but these papers date and identify the emerald. Your ancestry is Greek, right?"

My mother read the papers over my father's shoulders. "It is."

"Then I assume you've heard of the Necklace of Harmonia."

Mom gasped. "No!" She thumbed through the papers in Dad's hands. "It can't be. The necklace was lost a long time ago."

"As a whole," Liam said, "but it survived in pieces."

Mom's face lost all color.

"What is it?" I asked.

Liam inhaled. "Made of gold and jewels, the clasp two open-mouthed serpents, the necklace was forged by Hephaestus, a blacksmith god, as punishment. His wife, Aphrodite, had had an affair with Ares, the god of war."

Jack's arms tightened around me, his voice steady when he added, "It pissed him off, and Hephaestus offered the necklace to Harmonia as a wedding gift."

Mom sucked in a breath, and her brows creased. Because of her heritage and her age, Mom knew things about history most of us would have to research to find out.

"Harmonia was the daughter born of Aphrodite's affair with Ares," she continued. "The necklace was cursed to bring misfortune to all who owned it. It starts by causing small, overlooked mishaps, but in the end, it destroys its owners and their families."

"Why couldn't the Court detect it?" Leda asked.

"It was forged by a god to curse other gods," Mom answered, her voice awed. "Created with very ancient magic, the necklace was formed using a protection spell that made it undetectable. Otherwise, it never would have been worn by the gods, queens, and princesses Hephaestus wanted to destroy."

"A lot of supernaturals would pay big money to own it," Liam said, a mischievous glint in his eyes. "There are collectors who would do anything to break the protection spell and emulate it."

My father's hands fisted around the papers in his hands. "As dangerous as it is, you want me to hand it over to you? How many buyers do you already have lined up?"

"You really think I'd sell it?" Liam snorted. "In the wrong hands, that jewel could cause a lot of problems for all of us. I've already contacted the Court. I'm handing it over to them."

"You expect us to believe that?" my sister asked.

"Leda!" I gasped.

"It's okay," Jack whispered in my ear, his warm breath sending shivers down my spine.

"I'm not asking you to trust me," Liam told us. "As soon as you let me know where to find the jewel, a member of the Court will meet me there. I'm just the one transporting it."

"Why you?" Dad asked.

"Because the jewel doesn't affect hellhounds. Not in the typical way. You've seen what our stare can do for those under its influence. That's why Cressida getting to know my son when she did turned out to be a good thing. For them both."

"How?" Leda asked.

"Because Jack kept this from turning into a big problem for this town," Liam replied. "Not only because he was invested in protecting Cressida, but because *I* was invested in protecting him. Owning the jewel would cause just as much misfortune for hellhounds as it would you, but because hellhounds are forged from the same fires that created the jewel, the dark curse attached to it can't physically inhabit us. Besides," Liam shrugged, "I may have a hidden agenda."

"Pops!" Jack exclaimed.

His father smiled, but it didn't quite reach his eyes. "I moved my boys and my business to Havenwood Falls because it provides protection for my men and their extended families, a safe place away from my outside business ventures. The stronger this town is, the safer my club is from my enemies. If the Court can crack that protection spell and add it to their already strong wards, I'm a hundred percent behind it."

Liam inclined his head at my father. "Good job, Wieland. You may have brought something potentially disastrous to your family into this town, but you're getting the chance to turn it over to a greater cause." Sarcasm dripped from the biker's words, his smile hiding a warning I didn't miss. If my dad didn't turn over the jewel, Liam wouldn't have any problem taking it from him.

"This will stop if we hand it over?" my mother asked. "There's nothing else we have to do? No fighting?"

Liam swore, his gaze flashing to Jack. "What is it with people wanting violence today?" He snorted. "That's all you got to do. You'll be passing it and the curse on to the Court. They'll deal with it from there. There are some scary sons of bitches on that Court. I wouldn't worry too much about them or us."

Wieland swallowed hard. "It's at Summit. Take it. I just want it away from my family."

Liam pushed away from the wall and clapped my dad on the back. "See? Quick and painless. Let's ride." His gaze flicked to Jack, and then to me. "I'm guessing you're staying behind?"

"Yes, sir," Jack replied.

Liam studied us—his son and the small nymph with badly chopped off hair and no boobs—and he smiled. "You might want to think long and hard before you take on my hardheaded son, Miss Manos, but if you're up to the challenge, you'll have the club at your back."

With those words, he left.

My father followed him out the door, pausing long enough to mutter, "That may be easy for him to say, but I might have to give this some thought."

Mom shooed him away.

Leda stretched, moaning, and then popped her fingers. "Well, that was enough excitement for me. I need a shower and a change of clothes, so I'm out. I may even take the day off."

"To spend with your girl?" Mom asked hopefully.

"Mom!"

"At least give us a name. Just a name," Mom begged.

Leda paused. "Nikita . . . but, Mom, I don't really know how she feels about me. It's more like I'm into her right now, so no dinner or marriage plans, okay?"

"Fine." Mom waved her hands at the door. "Go!"

With a winsome smile, Leda disappeared. Dawn was coming, the day ahead now full of new possibilities.

Mom's attention turned to Jack and me.

"Nope," I said. "I'm grabbing a quick shower, a change of clothes, and then we're out, too."

Mom's face fell. "Okay, but," she touched the ends of her hair, wincing, "maybe stop by Shear Magic while you're out. Once they open."

"Time me!" I told Jack, pulling free from his embrace to make a run for the stairs. "If I'm not done in ten minutes, we're probably stuck here."

He grinned and started to count, "One, two, three . . ."

"Use your phone," I called down, halfway up.

"It died. Six, seven, eight . . ."

A quick shower had never felt so good.

CHAPTER 20

JACK PETERS

HOURS LATER

*F*or the first time since meeting Cressida, it was just me, her, and no agenda. Bright light poured into Apex Art Studio from the street beyond, the smell of wet clay thick on the air as Cressida took a seat at the potter's wheel, an unformed lump before her.

Across the room, she'd set up a group of tables and a myriad of art supplies. At each seat, a ceramic piece rested, the white surface clean and ready to paint, a "Happy Birthday" sign hanging from the ceiling above.

"Have you ever done this?" Cressida asked.

"What? Art or pottery?"

She laughed, patting the stool behind her. "Try with me."

If you'd asked me a week ago if I'd ever be found dead at an art studio shoving my hands in wet clay, I would have said hell no. Now, standing here, I still found it hard to believe. And yet, something about the smell and sight of it felt like possibility. Like the beginning of a journey I never would have thought to take on my own.

"I'm going to be really bad at this," I warned, dragging a second stool over. Settling in behind her, I braced my long legs on each side of her, my arms falling over her head. Her shorn curls, the strands recently cut at the salon in town, teased my chin as I leaned forward.

She took my hands in hers, lining them up. Compared to hers, mine were huge, and I marveled at the difference.

"They're stronger than they look," Cressida whispered.

"What?"

"My hands," she replied. "They are much stronger than they look."

With one fluid movement, Cressida started the potter's wheel, placing our hands against the clay. She molded it expertly, the material cool against our fingers, my chest pressed against her back. I rested my head on her shoulder, my breath mingling with hers.

"What does the tattoo on your chest represent?" she asked me suddenly.

Watching our clay-covered hands, I whispered, "The beast in me, and the three things he feels most defines him."

She turned her head, her gaze catching mine briefly before returning to the clay. "What defines him?"

There was something hesitant and uncertain about the way she asked me, and I found my lips curling in response, the need to reassure her so strong, it nearly knocked me off the stool.

"First," I answered, "is the tomb—this need to be near the dead, to help the souls of those passing on. The tomb is where his mother is, and while for most people that's a sad place, for his mother it's safe and warm. The same way it will be for me someday."

My hands abandoned the clay, my wet fingers running over her fingers, entwining and then disentangling. Learning. Feeling. "Second, there's the tree of life, its canopy connecting the beast to the sky, its roots connecting the beast to the ground. Reminding him that you can exist in two places at once."

Turning my head, I placed a gentle kiss on her neck, my lips moving over the healing wound the scissors had left behind on her skin. "And finally, there's the ship at full sail, moving over choppy waves. There's a quote that says, 'A smooth sea never made a skilled sailor.' The ship reminds the beast to learn from his mistakes, to take them for what they are: just another wave to break through."

I had completely abandoned the project before us, my clay-covered hand coming up to cup her face, my free hand sliding along her skin just under the hem of her shirt. I didn't dare go any higher.

"I'd like to try this," I said suddenly, surprising myself.

Cressida's head turned, our faces so close, our noses brushed. I liked hugging her from behind. If I leaned over far enough, I could fold her into me, keeping her safe forever.

"Try what?"

We were whispering, our breaths mingling.

I swallowed. "Being in a relationship."

Her eyes widened, and I could make out brown specks among the green in her gaze, a light line of blue tracing the center. Earth, water, and wind. My eyes were the fire.

"I—" she began, but I silenced her with a kiss, my lips tasting hers. Long, deep, and searching.

When I pulled back, she was breathing hard.

"That was in case you decided against a relationship."

"Why would I decide against it?" Cressida's newly short hair matured her features, widening her eyes and thinning her face, and I brushed a kiss on her clay-marked cheek.

"Hellhounds have bad tempers, we're incredibly hot-natured, we're possessive, and . . . our women often die in childbirth." I added the last one quick, almost as an afterthought, my lips spitting out the words.

Cressida froze. "What?"

"It's just something you should know. Not that you're considering marriage or kids. It's just that . . . I've never taken a girlfriend because I didn't want to get attached. Getting attached means possibly losing her one day. I think if we date, I may get attached."

For a long moment, Cressida stared, not saying anything. "Is that how your mom—"

I nodded.

"Oh."

My gaze dropped. "Hellhounds are tough. My brother likes to say we're badass. I don't know about that. I think we have the same vulnerabilities as everyone else. If I'm being honest, I think we have more. Or at least I do. I'm afraid of things. I'm afraid what will happen if I shift one day. I'm afraid of what being a part of my father's club may mean. *If* I decide to prospect in. I'm afraid of falling in love, because I'm scared losing the person I'm with will make me hate death." I snorted. "Which is another reason not to date me. I like cemeteries. Candlelit dinners in graveyards probably aren't very sexy. Not to mention the danger. Your family accidentally stumbled into bad luck because of your father's hobby. My family goes looking for danger just because."

Cressida touched my face, running her thumb over the bridge of my cheek. "What do you see when you look at me?" she asked.

"Cressida," I answered, and then, "you are absolutely beautiful."

She grinned. "And that's why the rest of that doesn't really matter . . . yet. We can take it one day at a time. Moment by moment. I've seen myself in a mirror, Jack. I like who I am, but I know what other people think of me, too. If you see beauty, then that means you're seeing more of me than most. I'd like to try the relationship thing, too."

"Thank God," I groaned.

Our lips fell together, a new promise sealed the way it should be.

Things could change between us. Especially if I joined SIN or if one of us went away to college, but right now, in this moment, I was proving her right. She told me I'd fall in love with her.

I wouldn't call this love yet. Mostly deep interest. We hadn't known each other long, but I had a feeling I was going to fall very, very hard.

The kiss ended, and I stared at her, no sunglasses between us, my eyes saying what my lips couldn't. Not yet. This was still too new.

If you're with me, I will protect you.

EPILOGUE

CRESSIDA MANOS

A WEEK LATER

*B*eing the sudden girlfriend of a hellhound had its advantages. Mainly that no one, and I mean no one, had the courage to mess with me. It also kept people from asking questions. No one bothered me about the weird things I'd done the week before. No one dug into the mystery about my family, even though the appearance of Court members at our jewelry shop when they confiscated the jewel must have raised eyebrows. Even the gossips left us alone.

Jack and I had been lucky. I'd heard stories about things that had happened in Havenwood Falls—things that had been covered up, but that most of the supernaturals ended up hearing about anyway. Many of them were tragic, with huge fights and lots of complications. The start of our relationship was a lot less dramatic compared to that.

For me, the solution to my problem had been a bad boy with a bad reputation, the beast he was afraid of and his very scary father the answer to my family's problem. We'd been saved before anything truly dreadful could happen.

I hated the jewel that caused it all, but it had also introduced me to my first love. At least, I was pretty sure I loved him. No way in hell I was telling him that, though. He'd probably run before he gave this relationship thing a chance. And I wanted desperately to give it a chance.

The sound of cats hissing and yowling pulled me out of my thoughts, and I grimaced, my hands quickly deserting the cage they'd been stuck in before slamming the door shut.

There were some disadvantages to being with a hellhound, too. The most glaring one was the fact that cats couldn't stand them. It made my work at the animal shelter a lot more difficult.

"You could warn me before you show up," I called out.

Jack, sans sunglasses, rounded the corner, entering the cat area of the shelter, his combat boots thudding over the linoleum floor.

"I can't help it if they can't see what a good guy I am."

I arched a brow. "Maybe they're warning me away from you."

"They'd change their minds if they saw what your mom did to that Slink cat of yours."

I glared. Slink still hadn't quite recovered from the incident. She had developed a severe phobia of my mother, which was causing all kinds of stress at home. Namely that Slink was suddenly all about destroying Mom's things, and Mom felt too guilty to scold her for it. "That was low, Peters."

He grinned. "Take a ride with me, Manos."

"I'm working."

"Take her," a female voice insisted. Isa came into view, stuffed her hands into the pockets of her white lab coat, and smiled. Widely. "I've been telling her she needs to get out more. Like normal teenagers. All she does is work and volunteer. And it's not busy today."

Jack's head hung, his hand hastily shoving on a pair of sunglasses before he looked up.

Isa pulled back the sleeve of her lab coat, revealing her tattoo. "It's okay. I know better than to look in your eyes, hellhound."

He frowned. "You smell human."

"I am human," she admitted. "But I've got some extra special abilities. Tell your dad if he keeps parking so close to the back of the building when he makes deliveries, I'll be glad to show him some of those abilities." She grinned mischievously. "The cats really don't like you guys."

Surprised, Jack laughed. "I'm not sure you really want me to tell my pops that."

"Oh, no, I really, really do," Isa said. "Now scoot."

Jack laughed, then reached out to grab my hand. "You heard the woman, Manos."

We left the shelter, the two of us hand in hand when we approached his bike. Something told me that with Jack's connection to the motorcycle club, and his possible future with them, the way we'd met was just the beginning.

I was a little scared of our future. Getting to know Jack was one thing. Being in a relationship with him was going to be a whole different kind of adventure, and I had a feeling it was going to be a lot scarier than what happened with the jewel from the Necklace of Harmonia.

We hope you enjoyed this story in the Havenwood Falls High series featuring a variety of supernatural creatures. The series is a collaborative effort by multiple authors.

Books in the Havenwood Falls High series you might also enjoy:

The Fall by Kristen Yard
Awaken the Soul by Michele G. Miller
Fata Morgana by E.J. Fechenda
Forever Emeline by Katie M. John
Falling Deep by J.L. Weil

Stay up to date at www.HavenwoodFalls.com

ABOUT THE AUTHOR

R.K. Ryals is the author of emotional and gripping young adult and new adult paranormal romance, contemporary romance, and fantasy. With a strong passion for charity and literacy, she works as a full-time writer encouraging people to "share the love of reading one book at a time." An avid animal lover and self-proclaimed coffee-holic, R.K. Ryals was born in Jackson, Mississippi, and makes her home in the Southern U.S. with her husband, her three daughters, two playful cats named Delphi and Paris, and a coffeepot she honestly couldn't live without. Should she ever become the owner of a fire-breathing dragon (tame of course), her life would be complete. Visit her at www.authorrkryals.com.

ACKNOWLEDGMENTS

I am so thankful to be a part of the Havenwood Falls journey. Writing Jack and Cressida's story was an adventure I will never forget. Not only because I felt a kinship to these characters, but because I loved writing a love story that doesn't start off in a typical way. I have high hopes for these two characters in the future.

This story would not have been possible without our fearless leader, Kristie Cook. Thank you so much for creating a town that brings authors and characters together in a unique and amazing way. I am so grateful that you are a part of my life.

I am always blown away by the amount of people it takes to bring a story together. There are so many that I want to thank.

First, I have to thank my husband, whose patience and diligence is always such a support for me. This novella was written during a very chaotic time in our household, and he handled it all like a champ. To my daughters, who inspire me on a daily basis. I am truly blessed with amazing children. They have passion, determination, and resilience. Raising them to be the strong women I am watching them become humbles me.

A heartfelt thank you to my personal assistant, Christina Silcox. Not only does Christina assist me so much in life, she is a beacon of strength. I am amazed by everything she does.

To Melissa Wright, Jessica Johnson, and Amanda Engelkes, who are always letting me use them for a sounding board. Your input and your suggestions always mean so much to me.

A special thank you to a group of loyal women who have followed me since the beginning of my career. To my Archive girls and my

Scribes group. The dedication you have shown me is not taken for granted.

There are no words big enough to express how grateful I am to be a part of the Havenwood Falls family. Huge thanks and crushing hugs to the Havenwood Falls authors who let me borrow the wonderful characters that make this story so strong. To the rest of the Havenwood Falls authors for the characters they've created. This town is possible because of all of you.

A massive shout out to Regina Wamba for the beautiful cover art. You are seriously incredible.

To Liz Ferry and Kristie Cook for your amazing editing. You make these books so much stronger.

Finally, to my readers, you take my breath away. It means the world that you read my words. I am extremely grateful for your support on this insane journey full of crazy twists and turns. My love to you always.

HAVENWOOD FALLS HIGH

Blood & Iron

AMY HALE

A Havenwood Falls Young Adult Novella

Blood & Iron (A Havenwood Falls High Novella) by Amy Hale

Miranda Saunders has spent her sixteen years playing by the rules. She's known for her impeccable style, good grades, and overall positive influence in Havenwood Falls. But in the vampire community, she's an oddity. Born a vampire, from a situation deemed impossible, Miranda's origins are an enigma to everyone. When a photo surfaces that brings up questions about her long lost father, she is determined to find the answers. That search lands her directly in the path of trouble—fellow vampire Kai Reynolds.

Having recently graduated from Havenwood Falls High, Kai is tired of being told how to behave. Ready to break out of the mold he's been cast in by his parents and the town's supernatural leaders, he becomes a prospect for the SIN motorcycle club—something his parents loathe.

But when he catches Miranda snooping around the clubhouse, he has to choose: turn her in and prove his loyalty to the club, or help her find the answers she's looking for. If they work together, they're both taking risks far more dangerous than they understand. And the mystery surrounding Miranda's father is only the beginning.

BLOOD & IRON

AN EXCERPT

A bell rang. The loud clanging resonated from somewhere nearby. I was certain it was a familiar sound, yet at that moment, it seemed foreign. I couldn't register the meaning, only that it was annoying, and I wanted it to stop. I closed my eyes and rubbed my temples.

"What's wrong with you?" a grating male voice spoke near my ear.

I snapped to attention. "What?" I turned to find myself uncomfortably close to Gary Smithson, one of our notorious school bullies. His dark eyes stared back into mine. I placed a hand on his chest and pushed him away. "Nothing. I'm fine."

"You don't look fine. Are you on drugs or something?" He smirked, and I knew he'd just *love* to spread that specific piece of gossip around school.

"No, moron. I'm not on drugs. I have a headache. Now go away before I tell the entire school that you still sleep with a night light."

His eyes grew wide. "What? How . . ." He looked around and ran a hand over his brown buzz-cut hair. "You're suck a freak."

Then he strolled away, his stocky build shifting side to side as he pretended I hadn't just nailed his fear of the dark, which was common knowledge in vampire circles, or more precisely due to the vampires in those circles.

I sat at my desk a moment longer as the classroom continued to empty. I'd done it again. For the past several weeks I'd been having involuntary moments where my consciousness seemed to check out, like my body was present but my mind was elsewhere. Each time I found myself mentally transported, often surrounded by mist or fog, and I was always looking for something . . . or someone. I never found whatever it was, and it always left me feeling empty. I also woke from this odd trance with a headache.

I gathered my books and made my way to my locker, willing my head to clear before I had to face the rest of the day.

My best friend Zoey reached my locker about the same time I did. "I'm so glad it's Friday and only a half day. I'm already tired of this school year," she moaned.

I chuckled. "It's barely been a week."

"I know. I'm just over it already," she grumbled.

"One day you'll look back and wonder how it all went by so fast." I repeated the words I'd heard adults say dozens of times.

She rolled her eyes. "Hey, I've gotta help my dad at the shop for a little while after I leave here, but then I'm free if you wanted to watch a movie at my house or something." Her mood brightened significantly at the subject change.

"Uh, yeah. Sure." I dug through my purse, looking for my house keys.

"Are you okay, Miranda? You've seemed kinda distracted lately. And you look tired."

"Do I?" I glanced at myself in my locker mirror. I did look a little tired, although only those closest to me would have really noticed it. My shiny long blond hair was still perfectly in place. My makeup was flawless and accented my features impeccably. Looking amazing was just one of the perks of being a vampire. My eyes, though . . . the gold flecks that were scattered within the dark irises were usually luminous. Now they seemed dull and joyless.

"Have you been sleeping okay?" She placed a hand on my arm.

"Mostly. I seem to just randomly zone out a lot. And I've been having some strange dreams. Like I'm chasing something or being chased. For some reason, I've had a lot of anxiety off and on. It hits at weird times. I can't seem to shake it." It sounds odd, vampires sleeping, but my mom and I, we're not your average Gothic vampires. Truth be told, we're not average in any way.

I hadn't told anyone about the dreams, the anxiety, or the trances, but Zoey was my confidante. I could tell her anything. She knew my darkest secrets, like the fact that I was a vampire. And I knew hers, such as her being a dragon shifter. Those were the kinds of things you took to your grave when roughly half the population in your town was human.

"Want to talk about it?" She glanced at her watch, and I knew she needed to get to her dad's shop.

"We can later. I'll meet you at the store after I've dropped some stuff off at home." I gave her a quick hug.

"Great, see you in a bit." She dashed down the hall and out the front doors of the school.

I loaded my backpack with the books I needed to take home and slung it over my shoulder. It was a relatively nice day, and I was glad I'd left my old car at home. It hadn't been running particularly well, and I enjoyed walking, when the weather was nice anyway. The exercise gave me time to think, and this was a day I needed it more than ever.

I mulled over various issues as I walked, trying to decide which one might be the cause of the unsettled feelings I'd been fighting. I'd just celebrated my seventeenth birthday, but it wasn't a major milestone like eighteen or twenty-one. It didn't have the feeling of big changes and responsibility that I assumed would come with those ages. I hadn't seen a lot of my mother lately, but I assumed that was due to a heavy workload. Being a marketing analyst could be demanding work. Most of the time, she worked remotely, but now and then she had to travel to the main headquarters in Denver. I didn't even know what her company sold. It had something to do with computers or something. Whatever it was, it paid the bills. It was just her and me, and Mom worked hard to provide for us. I had no siblings, and I didn't even know who my father was. Mom didn't talk about him.

Nothing I thought of fit. I couldn't describe the feeling other than to say it felt like I'd lost something important. And that I only had so much time to find it before it was gone from me forever. It was ominous and frightening. Despite what the movies said, Gothic vampires couldn't see into the future or read minds. At least, I'd never met any that could. And although I wasn't a normal Gothic vampire, I still didn't think visions or trances were something I should be experiencing. It felt . . . wrong. So I'd been left with this void I didn't know how to fill, and disturbing episodes I couldn't explain.

I unlocked the door to my house and put my backpack on the kitchen table. I scribbled out a note for Mom letting her know I'd be with Zoey the rest of the day, then I locked back up and walked toward the town square and Simple Treasures Pawn Shop. I hadn't quite made it to Eighth Street when I heard a noise from behind me that sounded like thunder. I felt it as well. The ground vibrated beneath my feet, and before I could even turn around, my senses were telling me to be alert and careful. I looked back just in time to see three large men on motorcycles roar past me. They were wearing leather cuts with the Swords of the Infernal Night logo on them. SIN was their acronym, and it seemed to fit them to a tee. While they appeared to be ordinary bikers, something about them gave off a vibe that they were anything but. That ominous feeling intensified, and I was anxious to get to the pawn shop.

Purchase *Blood & Iron* wherever books are sold.

www.ingramcontent.com/pod-product-compliance
Lightning Source LLC
Chambersburg PA
CBHW051950170626
46808CB00007B/2546